ADULT DEPARTMENT

1. Materials are not renewable.
2. Fine Schedule
   - 1-5 days overdue .... grace period, no fine
   - 6-10 days overdue .... 25¢ per item
   - 11-19 days overdue .... 75¢ per item
   - 20th day overdue .... $2.00 per item
3. Damage to materials beyond reasonable wear and all losses shall be paid for.
4. Each borrower is held responsible for all materials drawn on his card and for all fines accruing on the same.

FOND DU LAC PUBLIC LIBRARY
COUNTY EXTENSION DEPARTMENT
FOND DU LAC, WISCONSIN

THE IMPOSTER

Also by Paula Sharp

THE WOMAN WHO WAS NOT ALL THERE

THE IMPOSTER

Stories About Netta and Stanley

Paula Sharp

HarperCollins*Publishers*

"A Meeting on the Highway," "Hot Springs," and "Books" originally appeared in *The Threepenny Review,* and "Hot Springs" also was anthologized in *New Stories from the South: The Year's Best (1989).* "The Imposter" first appeared in *The Harbor Review,* and "Piggly Wiggly" in *The New England Review.*

I wish to thank Steven Wasserman for his unflagging encouragement during the writing of this book. I also wish to thank Gina Maccoby for her continuing assistance; Terry Karten for her editorial suggestions; Margaret Diehl, Nancy Krikorian, Lesley Sharp, and Emily Wheeler for reading and criticizing the manuscript; Susan Brown for her careful copyediting; and Mark Kyrkostas and Diane Lopez for providing helpful information. I gratefully acknowledge the Barbara Deming Memorial Fund, the Geraldine R. Dodge Foundation, the New Jersey State Council on the Arts, Alfred and Martha Oxenfeldt, and Yaddo Artist's Colony for their generous support during the writing of *The Imposter.*

FIRST EDITION

Designed by Alma Orenstein

Library of Congress Cataloging-in-Publication Data

Sharp, Paula.

The imposter : stories about Netta and Stanley / Paula Sharp. —1st ed.

p. cm.

ISBN 0-06-016563-4 (cloth)

I. Title.

PS3569.H3435I47 1991

813'.54—dc20 90-56369

---

91 92 93 94 95 AC/HC 10 9 8 7 6 5 4 3 2 1

This book is for Lauren Austin-Breneman,
and for my sister, Lesley Sharp

CONTENTS

Joyriding: An Introduction 1

NETTA

The Imposter 23
Beaulieus in Wisconsin 41
Piggly Wiggly 75

STANLEY

The Golden Car 115
Hot Springs 131
Books 147
A Meeting on the Highway 163
Barbarians 173

JOYRIDING: AN INTRODUCTION

BYRON COFFIN'S venerable Wall Street firm had entrusted him with the defense of Dr. Charles Eklund, a prominent Long Island obstetrician recently arrested for practicing without a license. All through August of 1978, Byron worked until eleven o'clock at night, and then took a limousine home to New Jersey. He would have preferred a taxi, but the firm paid for a car service. The ostentatiousness of riding in a limousine secretly embarrassed him. However, he found that the hour of leisure gave him the opportunity to reflect on recent changes in the law, and to prepare for meeting his wife, who was considerably younger than Byron and had become difficult to please over the years of their marriage. She had evolved into a chronically anxious, frazzled person, and sometimes Byron wished that he had remarried a woman his own age, whose personality would have been well-formed and dependable.

"When I first met you," she had told him that morning, "you seemed so different. So witty and debonair, somehow. Not so stiff, somehow." She had stared at him, as if trying to conjure that image of him but evidently failing in her efforts. "Do you know that you rarely even talk? That speaking with you is like pulling teeth?"

What could he say? He had certainly never led anyone to believe that he was debonair or an avid conversationalist.

Then she had spoken a terrible and unkind exaggeration. "It's like being married to a dead person!" She had grabbed her briefcase, and exited the house without saying good-bye. Byron was not looking forward to returning home that evening. Perhaps he should have worked an hour later. No doubt his adversary, a young woman fresh out of Columbia Law School, was burning the midnight oil at O'Melveny & Myers.

Byron waited longer than usual for the limousine. Around 11:30 the driver appeared and displayed his number on a square of cardboard. Once seated, Byron opened his briefcase, switched on the reading lamp attached to the back dashboard, and arranged several papers on top of the case. It seemed that Dr. Eklund had once been charged with bigamy in New Jersey. The SEC was also investigating Dr. Eklund's role in the sale of several hundred thousand dollars' worth of penny stocks in a company called Miragem Tungsten.

Byron missed his early days as an assistant district attorney. He briefly imagined prosecuting his own client. "Oh come now, Eklund, do you expect this jury to believe such a hodgepodge of poorly told lies, badly concocted alibis, and saintly explanations for shady acts?"

"Objection!" some poor defense attorney would call.

"The question needs no answer. Withdrawn," Byron would follow cleverly. But then, Dr. Eklund had convinced countless people to trust him. It was incredible to Byron that anyone could be so easily fooled. Perhaps some human beings just secretly desired to be taken in.

The limousine halted abruptly, and Byron's papers leapt to the floor.

"Dawg," the limousine driver explained.

On Wall Street? Byron wondered. But then a German shepherd, perhaps an escaped guard dog, rushed under his window. Byron retrieved his papers. On the limousine floor was an empty bottle of Boone's Farm strawberry wine. When he recounted the story of the limousine ride later, Byron Coffin would remark that the wine bottle, and two other details, should have alerted him to the danger of his position from the beginning.

The first such detail was that he did not recognize the driver, although the limousine company was a small, well-established enterprise, which rarely introduced new chauffeurs. Byron would have remembered this driver, because he was such an extraordinary individual. Even seated, he impressed as an uncommonly tall person, well over six feet. His height was accentuated by a narrow frame and sticklike arms that extended several inches from the cuffs of his jacket. Moreover, even in the middle of the dramatic events that followed, the driver rarely said anything: he appeared to be more reserved an individual even than Byron. When the driver did finally speak on his own behalf, he had such a mumbling southern accent that Byron found him difficult to understand. Later, however, the driver's speech seemed to have a foreign inflection, as if he were trying to disguise his origins. Thereafter, Byron detected a definite New Jersey accent. Was the driver a foreigner who had not yet arrived upon an American accent of choice?

The other immediately notable fact was that the limousine driver's girlfriend rode in the seat next to him, a circumstance which violated the implied duty of privacy owed to any limousine fare. This girlfriend did almost all of the talking for the driver, after introducing herself as Antoinette.

"But you call me Netta," she had added, as if she expected Byron to engage in conversation.

Shortly after he noticed the wine bottle, Byron sensed that Antoinette was staring at him, no doubt summing him up: Byron was aware that he was a stuffy-looking man past his prime, dressed in the gray suit and pale yellow tie that had become the acceptable fashion of the day.

When he looked up from his papers, Antoinette said, "I hope you don't mind if I ride along with Stanley here." She was a slim girl with black eyes like thumbtacks and dark hair drawn back in a rubber band. She smelled unmistakably of marijuana.

"Well," Byron said.

"Stanley's always telling me about his job, and I kept promising myself I'd come and see firsthand what it was like. So here I am."

"Well."

"Now I've been in one, I think these limos don't have much to them, do they? I own a Silverado myself."

Byron nodded.

"Are you going some place in particular?" Antoinette asked, presumably to be funny. Byron's secretary always called the limousine company ahead of time to inform them of his destination.

"To Montclair, New Jersey. Take the Holland and circumvent Jersey City. You do know the way?"

"Yep," the driver answered.

"Fine," Byron told him.

As Byron Coffin had noted, the driver, Stanley, was a taciturn person. Nevertheless, he had a rich inner life never accurately reflected in his speech. After answering Byron, Stanley thought to himself: On a clear night like this, Jersey City, the ugliest city in the world, glimmers like a diamond necklace stretched out on the banks of the black river.

Periodically, messages in grumbly voices issued from the car radio in the front seat: "Smashup on West Side Highway off Ninety-sixth Street" and "Martin Sealy in limo six fifteen has a dead battery, if anyone passing that way could give him a hand. Next time, turn off your lights, Martin!" There was even a report of a stolen limousine. "Please keep your eye out for Boris Wasserman's limo. It appears he has been the victim of a robbery and his limousine hijacked." The radio dispatcher sounded amused. He read off the limousine's number, but his voice was lost in static. "Car needed at O'Melveny and Myers in the midtown area." Byron looked up. Could that be his adversary, leaving so late?

Several events followed which should have further aroused Byron's suspicions.

A white limousine pulled up beside his, and the driver rolled down his window to talk to Byron's chauffeur. Antoinette called, "Duck, Stanley, don't let him see you." Byron thought that the driver of the other limousine registered surprise before Stanley stepped on the gas and maneuvered into the far left lane.

"You see," Antoinette said, laughing at her joke, "we really just picked up this limo on a joyride and we have to kind of lay low."

Byron nodded, but did not laugh. His wife criticized him for having no sense of humor. He thought of an uncle on his mother's side who possessed an embarrassing and off-color prankishness. The uncle had a continuing practical joke which had annoyed Byron throughout his childhood. The uncle would obtain a stack of crisp, unused twenty-dollar bills from the bank, and then he would align the stack, brush it along the left side with rubber cement, and glue the bills to the edge of an empty checkbook. When he paid for gas or meals, he would rip out one or two twenties, checklike, from the book, causing a flurry among gas station attendants and waiters who feared the bills were counterfeit.

The limousine approached a rather frantic-looking woman standing under a streetlight near Bowling Green. She appeared to be in her fifties, and was somewhat overdressed for Byron's taste. She called to a taxi ahead of them, but it barreled on. She continued to wave her hand, which was clutching a small red purse. As the limousine driver passed her, Byron distinctly heard her cry, "Oh God, none of them are stopping! They aren't stopping!" He returned to his paperwork.

"Stanley, maybe we should go back and get her," Antoinette said.

As Byron read, he felt the limousine make a sharp turn,

which extended into a U-turn. He looked up, and saw the same woman ahead of the limousine. The car slowed. It stopped. Antoinette opened the door.

"We're not supposed to pick up customers, except by prearrangement, ma'am," she said. "But you looked so worried out here, we thought we might be able to give you a lift."

No, you certainly are *not* supposed to pick up customers off the street, Byron thought.

"Oh, thank you so much!" the woman said, opening the door on Byron's side, so that he had to move himself and his papers to the left, and adjust the lamp perched on the back dashboard. The smell of bath powder filled the limousine as the woman closed the door. Bath powder and fingernail polish remover. She wore a dress of a synthetic material, low-cut and brightly colored. Byron guessed that she was an executive secretary.

"I'm Mrs. Dupont," she said, turning to Byron.

"Coffin," he answered.

"What?" Mrs. Dupont asked, looking almost fearful.

"My name is Mr. Coffin."

"Oh, oh I *see*." She laughed.

His wife had told him that morning, "Coffin, ha. Talk about the shoe fitting."

"It's so desolate in this area at night," Mrs. Dupont said.

"I know what you mean," Antoinette answered. "I would take a bad neighborhood any day over Wall Street. It's downright creepy around here at this hour. I don't see how people can work in this neighborhood."

"Oh, I don't work on Wall Street, heavens no. I've never earned a dollar in my life." Mrs. Dupont smiled as if proud of this fact. "I came down here to visit my brother in Beekman Hospital."

"But Beekman's quite a few blocks from here," Byron answered.

"None of the streets have numbers and they all criss-cross each other." Mrs. Dupont waited, as if expecting Byron to ask something else. She then stated, "My brother has a tumor in his stomach the size and shape of a monkey's head."

The driver Stanley thought passionately: Thank God I stopped for you!

However, he merely nodded as he turned onto West Street.

"I'm sorry to hear that," Antoinette told Mrs. Dupont.

"I walk from Beekman Hospital to the World Trade Center every day and take the PATH back to Hoboken. But today I had to wait until after nightfall while he was undergoing these horrible tests. I just got turned around somehow in the darkness."

You certainly did! Byron thought.

"We're on our way to Jersey right now. Can we ride you over?" Antoinette offered.

"Actually," Byron interceded, "we'll be taking the Holland Tunnel by way of Jersey City and not the Lincoln Tunnel."

"That's quite all right," Mrs. Dupont said, patting his hand as if he were the sick one. "You can just drop me off at the World Trade Center." She looked out the window and drifted away, seemingly forgetting that he was there.

But then she turned to him and asked, "Have you ever been in a hospital?"

"Just once, when I suffered a concussion." Byron did

not mention that his doctor recently had recommended that he enter the hospital for cardiovascular tests. Byron was well aware that the medical system had a pecuniary interest in subjecting consumers to unnecessary and intrusive procedures, and he doubted there was anything wrong with him.

"You were in an accident?"

"A freak accident, yes." He did not elaborate. Byron thought of adding that he had been visiting his children from his first marriage, and had been struck by a piece of metal flying off a Ferris wheel at a North Carolina amusement park, but he realized the anecdote would reveal too much of his personal history. Far too much. It would require a long explanation of something for which he had no explanation. Even he had trouble believing that he had an ex-wife and children.

Mrs. Dupont appeared to be waiting for more information.

"In any case I recovered."

She gave him a searching look.

Byron averted his gaze. Shortly afterward when he glanced back at Mrs. Dupont, she appeared to be on the verge of tears. "Please contain yourself!" he wanted to order her. He dealt with women like this all week: overperfumed secretaries who always seemed to be talking on the telephone about a mother's illness, or a rebellious son or the fathers of their children.

"I know in my heart of hearts that Russell—my brother—will recover too! They're going to blast that tumor with chemotherapy and they say it could all but vanish in only three sessions. Then they do thirteen more just to make sure it doesn't dare rear its ugly head again.

They're horrifying it back to wherever it came from. He just happens to be in excruciating pain in the meantime."

Byron knew what would happen next, and it did: an outburst.

Mrs. Dupont turned to Antoinette. "It's not my brother!" she wailed. Byron thought he had misunderstood her, but then Mrs. Dupont said, "It's another man! I've been seeing him six months." She made an effort at self-restraint, wiping her eyes and sitting up straight. "Don't get me wrong," she said, placing her hand yet again on Byron's arm. "I was faithful to my husband for twenty years and I expected to be for twenty more. Then, all of a sudden, there I was in love with a man I met on the PATH train! We're head over heels! I lead a double life now, like Mr. Jekyll and Mr. Hyde. I'm ordinarily a very sane, sensible woman, Mr. Coffin."

"Doctor."

"What?"

"Of course you meant *Dr.* Jekyll and Mr. Hyde," Byron corrected her, but he noted an unintended consoling tone in his voice. Mrs. Dupont seemed satisfied.

"And the terrible thing is, I can't even visit him in his hospital room, because his wife would know. I sit in the waiting area for hours and hours just hoping for a member of his family to walk by discussing him. I hear them in his room, talking in low voices to each other. I feel like a criminal, having to hide like that! Imagine not being able to be with your loved one at such a time, because what binds you is a secret, and if you break the secret, you'll be torn asunder."

Until this juncture, the driver Stanley had been concentrating on his route and the milling traffic, but he felt

Mrs. Dupont's anguish pulling him into the dialogue in the backseat. It's so hard to live in secret, he thought. It makes life full of danger. Like, for example, you go to a hotel with a lady during an affair. Neither of you can tell your loved ones where you are. So that if something happened to you—the hotel burned down or you were robbed or you both got food poisoning, say—no one would know where to find you. It is a fact that every secret you have turns you into a kind of secret, and hides you away until you become almost invisible, like a ghost.

Stanley told Mrs. Dupont, "I'm sorry to hear that, ma'am, it's a crying shame."

Byron looked out the window.

"That's a terrible position to be in," said Antoinette. "Believe me, I know. You have to hope he senses that you're there, worrying about him. But why couldn't you just walk in his room and say something to him quick and then walk out? Then you could act like you made a mistake, and leave fast, but he'd see you."

"Does he work at an office somewhere?" Byron heard himself say. "Could you pretend to be an emissary from his friends at work, perhaps deliver him a big flower arrangement with a note from the office?" Byron was surprised at himself, but he continued with some pleasure. "I am certain that is the procedure in my law firm under such circumstances."

"Why, it's an idea," Mrs. Dupont said, looking at him with curiosity. "I'd never arrive on a thing like that. My. It just might work." She smiled at Byron.

The limousine parked outside the World Trade Center. Mrs. Dupont opened her purse and pulled out a ten-dollar bill that had been folded neatly into a brown wallet. "Please," she said, handing the bill over the seat.

"I'm sorry, ma'am," the driver said. "We can't take but tip money." He handed back the bill.

Byron knew for a fact that tips were included in the limousine fare: drivers were not supposed to carry money of any kind, in order to avoid the risk of robbery.

Mrs. Dupont took out her coin purse. "Well, here then," she said, retrieving a generous amount of change. "Thank you very much for service beyond the call of duty."

As she slid out of her seat, Mrs. Dupont said to Byron, "It's been a pleasure. I forgot to tell you my first name. It's Roxanne."

"Byron," he answered, raising his arm to shake hands.

"What a lovely, romantic name," said Roxanne, taking his hand. When she closed the door, Byron felt inexplicably, utterly alone.

I wonder, Stanley thought as he drove away, whether the police are on the lookout for me yet. I sure do need gasoline, but I'd better wait until I get to Jersey City to tank up.

• • •

After this incident, the New York County Office of Probation would prepare a presentence report which described Stanley's actions that night as follows:

Indictment/Charges:

Attempted second degree (felony) murder
attempted first degree kidnapping
first degree robbery
third degree robbery

criminal possession of a controlled substance in the seventh degree
operating M.V. while license suspended
leaving scene of accident without reporting (2 counts)

Description of Offense:

Defendant Stanley Beaulieu was superficially cooperative during our interview, volunteering little information and answering all questions from this officer with a simple "yes" or "no." When questioned as to his motive for the crime defendant stated only, "I love cars."

Defendant admitted that he took the limousine from the driver and then drove all night, collecting and discharging passengers, and receiving several large tips although he reportedly did not receive a tip from the complainant Coffin. Defendant states that, at Coffin's request, he drove said complainant through the Holland Tunnel. At approximately 11:42 p.m., defendant winged a horse trailer in the tunnel and he fled down the median. The Jersey City police pursued him for several miles until he veered off the road to avoid striking a station wagon belonging to the convent of Assumption/All Saints on Pacific Avenue, where he was apprehended. Defendant has been charged with resisting arrest by the Jersey City police.

Victim Impact Statement

Complainant Coffin remains in the hospital and was not available for interviewing. Coffin was questioned briefly by the police at the crime scene, at which time he stated that a second person, Roxanne Dupont of Hoboken, had also been picked up under false pretenses by defendant. However, a police check of Hoboken residents reveals no one by that name.

The limousine's owner, Boris Wasserman, reports that his vehicle was only slightly damaged. Wasserman related that at approximately 8:02 p.m., he was on duty in the midtown area, when a young man approached him, and produced a T-shirt wrapped around what appeared to be a pistol, although he may have simulated holding a gun. The young man stated, "This here is a robbery and I'll take the car." At Wasserman's request, defendant did not take his personal money or wallet. Wasserman, however, due to the seriousness of the event, feels that defendant should receive the maximum punishment allowed by law. Wasserman reports that he saw defendant pick up the co-defendant in the limousine one block from the crime scene after the robbery had been completed. He believes she aided in the robbery, although she has not been indicted for this offense.

Complainant Karl Gustave Spanbauer reported that defendant fled the scene of an accident which damaged both a horse trailer belonging to Spanbauer and a Cutlass Supreme driving in the lane ahead of defendant.

Co-Defendant's Statement

Co-defendant Antoinette Henry [D.O.B. 5-12-58] was not cooperative. Although this officer attempted to contact her by telephone on numerous occasions, she did not return his calls. Miss Henry pleaded guilty to possession of marihuana and disorderly conduct, and received a fine. Charges for obstructing justice remain pending against her in New Jersey.

Defendant's Legal History and Social Background

Defendant, reportedly born in Raleigh, North Carolina [D.O.B. 7-18-59], was nineteen years old at the time of the crimes charged, and has a long criminal history including juvenile arrests for burglarous activities, joyriding and naked possession of a weapon. He has used several aliases including Stanley Shipley, Stanley Wilkes, Stanley Salazar, Wilkes Henry, Stanley Ray, Henry Ray and Ray Henry as well as Stanley Beaulieu. Defendant denies alcohol and drug abuse, although he admits to having smoked marihuana on occasion. Raised by his mother and grandmother, and various other relatives, defendant presently resides in Jersey City with the co-defendant Miss Henry, who is twenty years old. He is functionally illiterate and has no substantiated employment history. He reports that he drove a cab off the books for one year but this officer could not validate said report.

Evaluative Summary

This parasitic individual living with his paramour has no apparent means of earning a livelihood, little or no education,

> and lacks a supportive family unit. His prior probationary sentences have not deterred him from larcenous behavior. His prognosis for the future is extremely guarded.

A number of these facts erred: for example, Antoinette Henry was not Stanley's girlfriend, she was his second cousin, and they lived with her grandmother. Although Antoinette Henry was an inspiration behind the offenses at issue, the law does not codify the crime of inspiring an illegal act, and she was not an accomplice in any legal sense. And far from having weak family ties, Stanley Beaulieu, whose true name was Stanley Wilkes, felt himself to be overwhelmed and haunted by his family, past and present. He was also an excellent driver, and was not at fault in the accident in which the Cutlass Supreme edged over the double yellow line and spun into the back left fender of a horse trailer.

The truth is that when Byron Coffin entered the Holland Tunnel, there was little traffic visible in front of the limousine. A horse trailer driving at an annoyingly slow speed was directly ahead, followed by a handful of cars. Karl Gustave Spanbauer, the trailer's owner, had been born and raised in Dannemora, New York, a town dwarfed by the prison upon which its economy depended. He had worked at Clinton Correctional Facility for twelve years as a guard, a job which, in his opinion, differed little from being a prisoner. His only pleasure was raising Belgians: huge, chestnut horses with barrel chests and legs like tree trunks. Every year, horses he trained won championships at drafting competitions all over the Northeast.

In late August, Spanbauer drove to Wingdale, New York, to sell a yearling colt, and then headed south with a prize Belgian gelding named Oglethorpe to attend a drafting event in the Meadowlands. Spanbauer grew disoriented as he drove through Manhattan. He was unable to locate the Lincoln Tunnel. Eventually he found himself entering the flow of New Jersey–bound traffic through the Holland Tunnel.

As soon as Spanbauer entered the tunnel, Oglethorpe became outraged: he sensed the lack of air, the weight of the water above him, the circular walls constricting him. He kicked against the trailer's back doors like a man hammering on the door of his prison cell. From the cab, Spanbauer shouted at him to calm down, but Oglethorpe pulled against the rope that checked him until his halter snapped, and he continued to pummel the back door of the van. Spanbauer decelerated in an attempt to calm the horse: in his rearview mirror he saw a line of cars draw closer together, crowding toward his van. The cars' presence fueled Oglethorpe's bravery and ferocity. He reared once and kicked open the door. Spanbauer halted. The cars behind Spanbauer stopped. The head driver emerged shouting.

Oglethorpe leapt toward him, twisted in midair, landed on all four feet, and charged toward the steaming industrial air of Jersey City. As soon as he smelled the hot odor of asphalt traveling east from the refinery bordering Hudson County, and the humid, treeless atmosphere, Oglethorpe jackknifed and twisted back inside the tunnel, passed the horse trailer and the several cars slowly maneuvering around it, and headed toward the limousine and Manhattan.

Each person in the limousine saw something different. Byron Coffin saw the impossible: he looked at the horse but did not see it; even after hearing the thundering hooves and being blinded by the glorious yellow mane, he did not believe that a horse could be galloping through the Holland Tunnel. Byron placed his head in his lap and braced for a collision, after concluding that the golden whirl ahead of him was a vehicle out of control. He felt a terrible pain in his chest and thought he might be having a heart attack.

Antoinette did not brace herself: she leaned forward to witness such a fine spectacle more clearly. She saw a galloping draft horse, his massive legs hurtling him toward the limousine, his expression an alloy of joy and exhilaration and mischief.

Stanley also watched a Belgian thundering toward the car: he saw it clearly, its red nostrils flared, a horse bent on being something else, a monster or a rhinoceros perhaps, its gigantic hooves pounding the asphalt, its head lowered, charging through the traffic toward a silver Cutlass ahead of the limousine.

Once, on his eleventh birthday, Stanley's grandmother had driven him and his cousin down the wrong side of a six-lane divided highway. This had left Stanley with a permanent resistance to astonishment, and was one of several factors which had rendered him an accomplished driver with exceptional dexterity in emergencies. Stanley steered toward the center of the chestnut and silver whirling, aiming the limousine at the blank space he knew would appear between the horse and the Cutlass after the Cutlass had braked and spun across the yellow line. He and the two passengers heard a whoosh, a suspension of motion as if in the eye of a hurricane, and the limousine emerged, unharmed, and bore toward and beyond three police cars and out into the glimmer of streetlights at the mouth of the tunnel.

When Byron Coffin raised his head, he saw two police officers attempting to flag the limousine to a stop. The pain in his chest had become enormous, greater than he felt his body would contain. He slumped against the limousine door and thought longingly of Mrs. Dupont. Incredibly, the limousine passed the officers, and accelerated as sirens collected in a deafening, flashing blue and red array behind Byron.

Antoinette leaned over the seat and said, "Look, I better tell you something. See, Stanley used to drive this gypsy cab, so of course he carried a gun for night work, because being a taxi driver is a dangerous job and all."

She appeared to be unaware that Byron was suffering physically, and to mistake his expression for mental anguish. Her words made little sense to him.

"So one day he fell asleep in the cab, with the gun just sitting there in his pocket and the door open, and the police arrested him. Then they violated him and gave him a bullet."

Byron struggled to inject some sense into the situation. "They shot him because he had an unlicensed weapon?"

"No, no, a bullet means a yearlong sentence. You know, a bullet, like an ace in poker. They said he'd violated probation and then he had to serve a year in jail. He was on probation for a minor offense. So then, when he got out, he couldn't get a cab license anymore, because of the felony conviction. So today, see, when I pointed out this limousine to Stanley, with the driver just leaning against the car eating a sandwich, the motor running beside him, Stanley sort of borrowed this car."

Byron began to understand.

"You can see how this all could have happened."

Stanley, his foot on the accelerator, his attention on the police cars racing behind him, noted silently to himself that Netta's explanation was kind and not entirely honest. He had thought often about crime and believed that explanations based on an examination of the criminal's social background were always feeble. If you looked far enough inside a person, all you would find at the center was the plain and inexplicable thing he was as a child: *the Stanley in us* was what he thought to call it at that instant as he rounded the Quality Inn and raced down Manila Avenue. But, as the limousine dove under the railroad bridge at Sixth Street, Stanley speculated whether it might, however, be true that you could understand most crimes by sorting backwards through a person's history to find the one temptation he could not resist. You might then discover that temptation buried like a pearl at the center of his crime.

The limousine sped through the intersection at Newark Avenue and down the last stretch of Grove Street, turned and soared up Pacific Avenue past the Booker T. Projects and Curry's corner store. A red station wagon loomed ahead of Stanley like a terrible apparition. He stomped on the brakes, steering the skidding limousine past the station wagon and onto Pacific Avenue.

Byron heard sirens encircle the car. A police officer jerked open the driver's door and said, "It's the stolen limousine, the plates match, against the door or I'll break your arm!"

"Don't you hit him, you lousy bastards!" Antoinette yelled. "I'm not the only witness."

Byron could not move. It struck him fully at that moment that he was the victim of a kidnapping. His heart expanded in a new surge of pain. He tried to think of what to do, but the only idea which came to him was: Things like this do not happen.

The front door opened and Stanley, spread-eagled against the car, tilted his head down and asked, "Are you OK?"

Antoinette slid into the car seat from the opposite door, and lifted Byron's wrist while staring into his face. "Yes, you're breathing." Her voice was commanding and authoritative. "But you don't look good. Do you want to see a doctor?"

That was when Byron Coffin's heart stopped. At that juncture when he believed his life came to a close, Byron did not see himself from above as he floated over his own body; nor did he witness a blinding flash of white light and experience a state of bliss, as he had heard reported in accounts of those who had returned from death. He saw that his was a death without imagination. He simply thought: *I'm dead now.*

Thereafter, Stanley's face reappeared near the window. A thought surged in Byron's mind: he wished that he was this young man, tall and vigorous, or even Russell lying in pain in the hospital, and then finally he hoped simply to be Byron Coffin, or anyone at all. This was followed by a jumble of thoughts and desires before Byron sensed a sparkle of electricity, and a warmth that began in his toes. He felt his heart struggling into movement, fisting and unfisting painfully, maintaining its rhythm. Yellow light crept around the edges of things, and joy such as Byron had never experienced lifted and carried him back to the world of the living.

NETTA

THE IMPOSTER

HE HAD an anxious pink face and always wore a green suit, so that from a distance his head looked like a ham bone swimming on top of a pot of collards. Standing on the front step, Netta Henry could see his gray Valiant turning up Union Street and lurching forward with an air of expectancy. He worked as a college professor in Madison, but he knew a tenth as much as Netta's mother, who was a teacher's assistant at the elementary school. During the late summer and early fall of 1973, he drove up to Ripon, Wisconsin, every weekend and slept in her mother's bedroom.

"Mr. Morales is going to camp right here, Netta," her mother would say, pointing to a cot and pushing it into the far corner of her bedroom, twelve or so feet from the bed. "If the house was bigger, we'd have a guest room to put him in." Netta would roll her eyes at the implication that she could be so simple. She was fifteen, and if she had not made it with any boys, this was from lack of interest and not of opportunity. She was going to be the first woman priest or a political leader, and boys did not fit into her future vision of herself, a tall, solitary figure preaching from a pulpit or podium and utterly transforming all who heard her speak.

Netta's mother sat at the table near the kitchen window with her hands folded in her lap. She leaned forward when Mr. Morales's car snagged for a moment on a stump in the road. His head bobbed over the steering wheel, and the sunlight glinted in his face. Mr. Morales had a glass eye that was a piercing blue unmatched in intensity by his real eye. He also wore a toupee that rested inside the ridge of his hair, and he was so old that he had been a communist at a time when it was still stylish.

During Mr. Morales's earliest visits to the house, Netta had ignored him until he revealed to her that he had been a member of the Communist party in Spain. This detail had lent Mr. Morales an aura of mystery, so that Netta had taken a mild interest in him, and had even checked out *The Communist Manifesto* on his advice from the Ripon public library. She had been disappointed and indignant to find that the book contained a twenty-page preface written by the John Birch Society or a similar group. The preface began: "A specter is haunting Europe—the specter of communism. All the powers of old Europe have entered into a holy alliance to exorcise this specter . . ." She had scoffed at the inflammatory language, and returned this adulterated version to the librarian. She would have to wait to educate herself until she moved to a big city, like Jersey City, where her grandmother lived and where Netta intended to go as soon as she was old enough to escape Ripon. She did not discuss the incident further with Mr. Morales because her mother did not like to be reminded that he had been a communist.

"One thing I won't do around him is argue," Netta's mother told her. "He used to be a communist, and that's where he learned to argue the way he does. I'll tell you what he does: he takes what you say and pretends not to understand it. Then he argues with something you didn't say at all and you spend the rest of the time pointing out that he misheard you."

When Mr. Morales sat at their table wolfing down his food, he didn't listen to Netta's mother because he was too busy looking at her. Betty Henry was a small woman with frosted chestnut hair, and high breasts that bobbed under her blouse like hen's tails. When Mr. Morales tucked in his chin to accommodate his spoon without taking his eyes off Netta's mother, his toupee would move slightly forward like an animal poked by a stick.

Netta's mother had tried to get Mr. Morales to leave the toupee at home in the city. "I tell him, 'Sweetheart, you don't need to wear that thing to win me; you already won me,' and I just take it off and put it down next to us on the table." Netta pictured her mother slowly pulling the toupee off Mr. Morales's head when he was too far gone with kissing to resist.

Today, as the Plymouth came to a halt outside Mrs. Henry's doorway, Netta's best friend, Roberta, appeared from the other side of the street as if she had been lying in wait all morning for Mr. Morales. Before he began visiting, Roberta had never met a communist, although she was a year older than Netta and had lived in Detroit,

Milwaukee, Cincinnati, and Chicago. Roberta was the only person Netta knew who had resided in as many big cities as her cousin, Stanley.

Once, Netta had made a list of all of the places in which Stanley had lived:

STANLEY

1959–1962	Raleigh, North Carolina
1963–1964	Memphis, Tennessee, and Athens, Georgia
1964–1965	New Orleans, Louisiana (staying with grandmother)
1965–66	Montgomery, Alabama, and Miami, Florida
1966–1967	Little Rock, Arkansas
1967–1970	San Diego, California
1970 (summer)	New Orleans, Louisiana (staying with grandmother)
1970–1972	Reno, Nevada
1972 (summer)	Ripon, Wisconsin (staying with us)
1973	New Orleans, Louisiana (staying with grandmother)

Although Netta had been lucky enough to have been born in New Orleans and to have spent some time there, her father had moved the family to Ripon the summer before she started eighth grade. When he ran off to Canada less than a year later, Netta's mother had rooted herself in Ripon, as if without his help she could not find her way back into the world from a town with a main street three blocks long.

Netta would have given anything to trade places with her cousin, Stanley, or Roberta, whose father would be transferring to a new job in Indianapolis the following year. Roberta already had participated in civil rights marches and rock concerts, and habitually dressed in India cotton prints and other clothes never before imagined by people in Ripon. Today, Roberta was wearing a baby blue shirt tied at the waist to expose most of her belly. She had sewn some red flowered material in the shape of a hand onto the crotch of her cutoff jeans.

"Jim! Jim!" Netta's mother opened the front door and waved to Mr. Morales with such fierceness that she looked like someone trying to ward away a swarm of flies. Mr. Morales's real name was Juan de Dios, but he preferred to be called, simply, Jim.

He stepped out of the Plymouth with a dozen black-eyed Susans, and handed them to Netta's mother with a flourish. As he walked up the steps with her, he wavered for a moment, passing his hand over his eyes as if he felt like fainting. Mrs. Henry caught him around the waist and steered him into the house.

When Mr. Morales first started visiting, he often had blackouts over dinner. Suddenly he would stop in the middle of an especially long paragraph, bow his head, and press his slender, blue-veined fingers to his temples. The first time he did this, Netta had been impressed, and for two days she enumerated all the possible disorders to which the blackouts might be attributable: minor stroke, epilepsy, or even brain cancer. However, after a few weeks, Netta's mother had persuaded him to see a doctor, who concluded that Mr. Morales had anemia. Netta wondered that Mr. Morales presented this news with all the gravity of someone announcing that he was going to die.

At the table, leaning over his sweet potato pie with a funereal air, Mr. Morales announced, "I have anemia." At later moments, he would refer to his ailment with the same solemnity. In the middle of a story in which he recounted how the Falangist forces had destroyed the towns of Spain, his upper torso would begin to sway, he would draw his hand to his temples, and remind all present that he had anemia. Uttering the word with the same air of tragedy that imbued the names of mysterious and ravaged Spanish cities, he would pronounce: "Then it happened in Irun, Guernica, Bilbao, Santander, Anemia—I have anemia."

Initially, Netta had been interested in his accounts of the Spanish Civil War, often told in the first person. He had spent time in jail for participating in a demonstration against Franco in the late sixties. Netta's revisions of Mr. Morales's stories had been what originally attracted Roberta to him, so that now whenever the Valiant turned the corner onto their road, Roberta would invite herself to dinner. However, Roberta was growing impermeable to more knowledge. Mr. Morales taught Spanish history, and he had a tendency to lecture whenever he spoke on the subject. Roberta said that the longer she listened, the more difficult it became to pay attention to him.

"Netta, come on in and let's eat lunch together!" Netta's mother stuck her head out of the door. "You should get a bite to eat before you leave." Netta and Roberta were taking the bus to the city, where they would spend the night at the YWCA. As Netta went inside the house, Roberta slipped in behind her and seated herself at the lunch table. Mrs. Henry set an extra place for Roberta.

The black-eyed Susans occupied the center of the table so that no one could see the person directly opposite. Netta watched Mr. Morales, seated at her right, and from the far end of the table, Netta's mother could see only Roberta smirking as Mr. Morales spoke in his soft Spanish accent.

"On the way down here, I stopped to look at Mr. Shutz's farm. He's a very friendly guy," Mr. Morales began, the flowers ogling him with their ebony eyes. "Mr. Shutz showed me his new pigs, white hogs raised near where I grew up in Andalusia." Mr. Morales delicately raised a bite of ham to his mouth. Whenever he came to visit, he spent a third of his time talking to farmers near Ripon. He was doing a comparative study of Spanish peasants and Wisconsin farmers, but Netta noted with amazement that he still had not discovered that there were no real farmers near Union Street. Almost all the land within walking distance had been bought out by agribusinesses. Mr. Shutz was a gentleman farmer whose own father had worked as an executive at the Jolly Green Giant factory in town.

"All pigs look the same to me." Roberta laughed behind the blind of flowers. "I'm a city girl." She rose to get a glass of soda out of the refrigerator, brushing against Mr. Morales on the way up and back. Netta noticed that although he continued talking, his gaze kept wandering to the red hand on Roberta's pants just as water flows to the lowest point possible.

After lunch, Netta's mother left for a walk with Mr. Morales, first telling Netta to be back from the city by Sunday evening. Roberta and Netta headed together toward the highway to hitchhike. They pocketed their bus money, and their true purpose in going to the city was not to visit museums and the Madison Zoo, as they had told their parents, but instead to find a free clinic where Roberta could get a shot of penicillin.

Netta and Roberta waited an hour on the highway. The girls stood in the middle of the road with their thumbs stuck out, but even when Roberta put one hand on her hip and pushed the other hip out in a suggestive way, cars and trucks whizzed past them as if they were not there. Only Mrs. Wallington, the town gossip, slowed down as she approached them in the enormous Winnebago that served as the Ripon Book Mobile. She leaned out the side window, peering at Roberta, and drove on.

"As long as we're parked out here, we might as well look at Mr. Shutz's prize white hogs," Netta said, imitating Mr. Morales's accent by speaking with the same inflection she had heard used by an actor playing a German officer in a war film.

Netta led Roberta toward a wood fence, to which Mr. Shutz had tied his three-legged dog. The dog leapt to the end of his tether, a harpoon thrown by an unseen hand. He landed a yard away from the girls, embedded his front foot in the mud and lowered his head, snarling at them. Netta walked by the dog without flinching, and saw Roberta out of the corner of her eye pussyfooting her way around the dog. They wandered along the fence to get a good view of Mr. Shutz's prize white hogs. The hogs were scattered about, stuck in the yellow spring mud. They looked like pearls set in a precious metal.

A sow flung herself onto her feet and pushed her nose between the bottom slats of the fence. The dog pulled back on the rope, whining and trembling.

"Look at that," Netta said. "Dogs are afraid of pigs. Take a dog that could bite a man in half, or chase a herd of cattle over the field, and the same dog is terrified of a pig." In witness to this proclamation, the dog remained standing with his neck stretched out at the end of the rope so that at least his hindquarters were as far as possible from the pig.

"Pigs have fangs," Roberta interjected.

Netta raised her eyebrows to show she found this statement of dubious validity. Although Roberta might have a *broader* knowledge of the world, Netta knew her own knowledge of things was more *profound,* especially in matters relating to the wheres and whens of all animals not found in large cities. "The ladies have teeth," Netta instructed, "and the men have tusks."

Roberta pretended not to hear. "Nobody's going to stop for us," she answered. "We might as well take the bus." Netta was disappointed because she never had hitchhiked before, while Roberta had done so many times.

• • •

The bus stop for the local was on the same corner that harbored the storm sewer where Netta had thrown the envelope. The envelope had arrived at the Henrys' just a few days after Netta had checked out *The Communist Manifesto* from the library. The envelope was inscribed with a Washington, D.C., return address but had a local postmark, and contained five pages of questions Netta had to answer regarding her age, the age of her wife and children, and how long she had been a member of the Communist party. She had laughed at the letter and never filled it out, but after the papers had lain for a day in her room she decided to dispose of them for her mother's protection.

Sometimes after that, Netta wondered if she might have a government file somewhere with a secretly obtained snapshot attached to it. The possibility that a townsperson might be watching her to take an identification photograph made her walk taller and dress more offensively, and instilled her with pride and fear. She told no one about the envelope, to keep from implicating her family and friends.

A blue and gray bus nosed up the hill on the highway, and stopped in front of Roberta and Netta, letting out a gasp of air like a great surfacing whale. Netta sat in the window seat. Roberta waved out the window to a man she did not even know, and then sat down.

The bus driver's broad back completely obstructed their front view. As the bus rumbled beneath them, Roberta tugged at the corners of her shorts so that they would not bite into her thighs. She looked without interest at the passing landscape, and then focused on her friend. Netta was wearing a Boy Scout bandanna that matched her khaki shorts. Her face, as usual, was unpainted, her long black hair uncombed, and her T-shirt half tucked in. Netta's tennis shoes clung perilously to ankles which had never known socks, and she had several cuts on her legs as if she had spent all night running through blackberry bushes. Her legs were long, but her chest was as flat as her back, and she still hadn't reached five feet.

"Sooner or later, you'll have to start arranging yourself before you go out," said Roberta. "You can't dress like a boy forever."

Netta pressed her face close to the window and watched a spotted horse brush against an electric fence and jump a yard upward. "Look at that, an Appaloosa! I've never seen an Appaloosa around here before, just in books."

"You're falling behind your age," Roberta continued. "You're fifteen and you have to start learning things about men so they can only take advantage of you now instead of later."

This was Roberta's favorite subject, and she continued to talk in the same vein even though Netta ignored her. Netta already knew that Roberta had made love with more men in Detroit than she had names for. During her one year in Ripon, Roberta had slept with four men: the twin Minnow brothers from Fond du Lac, Leroy and Lazarus; a forty-year-old photographer, Mr. Silky, who had artistic photographs of naked women all over the walls of his basement; and, most recently, Myron Buttone, who had given her the syphilis. A local doctor had refused to administer Roberta a shot of penicillin, but he had called her parents to give them a diagnosis of Roberta's moral character.

Netta was loyal enough to know that the doctor and Roberta's parents were *them,* and that she and Roberta were *us.* She therefore understood that she must accompany Roberta to the city for moral support if the two were to remain friends. However, whenever Netta thought of what Roberta had to go through to get syphilis, Netta saw the Minnow brothers in her mind, their narrow-set eyes staring at her out of their pale, identical faces. Roberta said they were exactly the same, right down to the shape and size of their uncircumcised peckers. Netta had never heard either of them talk, doubted if they could, and conveyed this doubt frequently to Roberta. Netta had not met Mr. Silky in person, but she knew Myron Buttone, and when Roberta first mentioned him, Netta immediately told her what every town resident already knew: he had intercourse with dairy cows. Roberta acted as if Netta were just envious of her friend's love life, but she stopped seeing Myron, though she still met with the Minnow brothers and Mr. Silky often enough.

Netta fell asleep in her bus seat, and she saw the Minnow brothers staring at her out of a blue haze. They swayed slightly from side to side as if keeping afloat by breathing through gills or brushing their fins against the water. As Netta drifted further into sleep, she saw that there were not two Minnow brothers, but four, and then an assembly of a hundred, all swaying and identical and facing the same direction like people listening to a speech, or like a school of fish. One of them nibbled her shoulder, and when she tried to brush it away, she woke to Roberta poking her arm and telling her that it was night and they had arrived.

They walked to the YWCA, and paid for two beds, in a room that looked like a military barracks. Roberta fell asleep naked in the only single bed available. Netta took the top half of a bunk bed over a girl named Vanessa who had golden hair that fell in ringlets as tightly coiled as pigs' tails. Vanessa introduced herself as a religion major at the university who was preparing for a six-month trip in a van, which would start in Madison and end in Tierra del Fuego, if she could get all the visas she needed.

After Vanessa had snapped off the light attached to their bed, Netta suspended her head upside down over Vanessa's mattress and said, "I know someone who works as a history professor at the university. His name is Mr. Morales and he used to be a communist." Netta found that her voice had taken on a bragging and ominous tone.

The bunk bed jiggled as Vanessa sat bolt upright. "Mr. Morales! That lounge lizard! You know him? Does he still go around telling everyone he's a communist and that he spent time in prison under Franco? You know the real story is that he was once put in jail after a demonstration, and his father, who's from some rich line of fascists, pulled strings and got him out in a half hour." Vanessa let out a giggle that sounded like silver quarters rolling down a flight of steps into a drain.

"He tells everyone he was a member of the Communist party because he thinks it's cool," Vanessa continued, lowering her voice to a whisper when someone in a neighboring bed said, "Shhhh!" "But the truth is he left his Spanish wife because she joined a feminist group. They don't have divorce yet in Spain, so he fled to the U.S. Then he got fired from the university for feeling up all the women students!"

Roberta, who was dead to the world, muttered in her sleep a few feet away from them without waking.

"Now he lives in an apartment near the school but he doesn't work because he's independently wealthy, his father sends him money. I know all about him because he tried to push a friend of mine into the corner of his office and kiss her, two weeks ago when he came to clear out his things from the History Department, and all she could think about was that toupee—"

"That isn't all!" Netta interrupted, adding to the story as easily as if she were already familiar with the details Vanessa had recounted. "He's got a glass eye too!"

"NO!" Vanessa screamed with pleasure.

"And it doesn't even match his other eye! It's the color of a Coke bottle, but his real eye is just kind of gray." Netta stuck her head in her pillow to muffle her laughter.

"Shut up!" a woman's voice yelled at them out of the darkness.

Vanessa tittered. "Good night."

Netta answered, "Sleep tight," but after napping in the bus all day, she could not sleep at all. When she closed her eyes, she saw Mr. Morales's blue one focused on her like a magnifying glass and she burned with indignation. She felt she should jump out of bed right then and catch the redeye bus to Ripon to warn her mother before it was too late.

In the corner of her mind, she could see her mother's broad, naive face smiling placidly on the diabolical countenance of Mr. Morales, who slithered around the cot leering at her with a lustful eye. Then Netta saw herself enter the bedroom with a shotgun, pointing at Mr. Morales like a long finger showing him the way out of the house and Ripon. All night she replayed in her head various sordid dramas in which Mr. Morales would sometimes fall on his knees vainly begging forgiveness, and at other times end up headless at the bottom of the stairs with Netta and her mother tearfully and innocently recounting his death to a beneficent policeman in a gold-buttoned uniform.

When Roberta came to wake up Netta the next morning, Netta was still lying open-eyed on the top bunk in her rumpled clothes. Vanessa was gone. Roberta led Netta down the street to a coffee shop, where they each had four doughnuts and a cup of hot chocolate. Netta hardly spoke all morning, but half-listened as Roberta counted off for her the signs of primary, secondary, and finally tertiary syphilis, for which they might have to amputate your leg like they did to a famous French painter. Netta did not even look at the magazines and brochures in the free clinic while Roberta was getting her shot. Only after the two girls had boarded the bus back to Ripon did Netta's mind finally relinquish the single thought preoccupying it and allow her to sleep.

When they arrived in Ripon, Roberta awakened Netta by shouting in her ear, "BOY, are you good company! I might as well have gone by myself." Netta did not answer, but Roberta followed her home. When they arrived at Netta's house, Mr. Morales and Mrs. Henry were sitting on the front steps drinking cognac in miniature glasses. Mr. Morales did not have on his toupee. His hand lay in Mrs. Henry's lap, and she playfully tugged at his fingers. She was wearing a pale blue dress with a Peter Pan collar.

Netta planted herself in front of them. "I know all about you!" she thundered at Mr. Morales. "I talked to a girl who went to the university. She said you aren't a communist and you're rich and you lost your job teaching because you sleazed over all the girl students even up to two weeks ago and you're married and you were only in jail for a half hour!"

Mr. Morales froze, his cognac suspended in front of his eye like an opera glass. Mrs. Henry's face drained of all its color, and she took a look at Mr. Morales, seeing him for the first time. Then she fixed her eye on Netta, as if trying to decide between the two of them, the man and the spectacle in front of her that was her daughter.

Roberta waited politely on the curb, watching.

"Netta," Mrs. Henry said in an emotionless tone. "You apologize to Mr. Morales. He's our guest and I expect you to be civil! I don't know what's gotten into your head!" Her voice cracked a little, and she jumped up and ran into the house, slamming the screen door loud as a gunshot. Mr. Morales opened the door and sidled in behind her.

A man passing on the street whistled and shook his head when he saw the red hand sewn onto Roberta's shorts. Roberta was leaning against a tree, and had one finger hooked in her front pocket.

"Wish that was my finger in your pocket," the man said, raising his eyebrows in an appreciative, complimentary fashion. Roberta winked at him.

"You go home! You go home right now!" Netta yelled, picking up a stick as if she were going to throw it at Roberta. "I've had enough of you for two days!" Roberta backed away.

"All right already, be nasty." Roberta walked briskly down the sidewalk. In a minute, she caught up with the man who had passed by, and Netta could see them gesticulating and tilting their heads back in laughter.

When Netta's mother emerged from the house half an hour later, her collar rumpled and her eyes red, Netta was sitting on the front steps with the stick still in her hand. Mrs. Henry took the stick and sat down a yard away from her daughter.

"He says you can't get divorced in Spain. You see, there's an explanation for everything, if you give someone half a chance. And he just went after those girls because he was lonely," Netta's mother added. "I never thought he was perfect, but right now he's the best there is." She looked at her daughter's profile, and then slunk back in the house with her head bent.

Netta stood up to speak from the podium of the top step, but suddenly she felt as if the lesson she had to utter could not bear repetition. She was glad to look around and find herself completely alone. There was no one on Union Street, or up on the field overlooking the highway where Mr. Shutz's hogs usually lay baking in their muck. Someone had unhooked the three-legged dog from his chain, and even the pigs had been taken in from their golden hilltop.

BEAULIEUS IN WISCONSIN

I'LL NEVER visit there again. Eight months of the year it's so cold you want to cry. Then in May, that snow starts to thaw, and with it melts the fermented cornmeal in the silos and the pig dung that's been gathering all winter. And the town stinks. For days on end, Ripon stinks like a dead man. They plow the big fields with their rackety machines and after that there's nothing but fields of mud stretching from horizon to horizon. Then the heat sets in, the pig corn rises, and for a few weeks if you drove through Ripon, you'd say, Look at that pretty little Wisconsin farm town, sitting there in amber waves of grain. But around August, the corn thrashers knock everything down, and for another month there's mud with gray, bent, and broken cornstalks stabbing into it. After that, the snow comes back like a boyfriend you've grown tired of who's always hanging around the house.

I never had any longing to go to an ice-cold place. But every few years when things got rough for my daughter, Betty, she'd send me a letter asking if I was lonely and wanted to stay with her. She kept pulling me farther and farther from my roots. First, she took me from Franklin to New Orleans. Then it was Baton Rouge when Manny got a teaching job there, and then it was New Orleans again, and then Shreveport for a year, and then Ripon and that's where I got off.

I ran away to Jersey City, a place you hear about if you're from nowhere, a sort of holy land for the rootless. I'd been safe in Jersey City for almost three years when I got a little lavender envelope addressed in perfumed ink to "Mrs. Viola Beaulieu." Inside was a card saying, "Dear Mama—It's just *breathtaking* here. I know you'd love it, and Netta and I would love to have you." What that letter said to the naked eye was plainly nothing. But that's only if you don't know "Netta and I" meant that man had skipped out on them. I had suspected for over a year from our phone conversations that he'd run off—I could tell because of this strained sound in Betty's voice that she gets when she's pretending.

Betty married a no-good man from Baton Rouge, Manny Henry. He thought he was God's gift to mankind, he was so smart, and Betty believed him. She was crazy about him. If you didn't know Betty well enough to look through her eyes, you wouldn't have seen much in Manny. He was a graduate student at Tulane, studying Cajuns. Now, here's how smart Betty is—she told him she was Cajun.

She started scattering French words into her conversations and pronouncing her maiden name with a foreign accent, instead of just saying *Bo-lee-oo,* the way we Beaulieus always have. She went on and on about how her grandfather Henri was a swamp trapper from Cameron, and how her grandmother never spoke a word of English and was killed by a water moccasin. Even after Betty had hooked Manny, she kept this up, and went so far as to hire a man to do a family tree, which she copied onto fancy paper and mailed to me after adding a few things:

?----------? ?------?

HENRI BEAULIEU----------ALINE, née?
(Cajun)
b. 1880
Cameron
(swamp trapper)
d. 1920

ALINE, née?
(Cajun)
b. 1887
New Iberia
d. 1938
from snakebite

HENRI
b. 1902
Morgan City
d. 1904
from malaria

ARTHUR
b. 1905
Morgan City
d. ?
(left with Milton for Texas, 1927)

MILTON
b. 1909
Morgan City
d. ?

DORIAN DAIGLE----VIOLA, née BEAULIEU
b. 1911
Larose
(Cajun? left for Tampico, 1942)

VIOLA, née BEAULIEU
b. 1912
Morgan City

LEROY RAY-------née BEAULIEU
b. 1888
Needmore, Texas
d. 1941

ARTHURINE, née BEAULIEU
b. 1913
Morgan City

EMMANUEL-HENRY---BETTY, née BEAULIEU
b. 1931
Baton Rouge

BETTY, née BEAULIEU
b. 1937
Franklin

GERTRUDE, née RAY---ROSS WILKES
b. 1935
Morgan City

ROSS WILKES
b. 1923
Raleigh, N.C.
(current whereabouts unknown)

ANTOINETTE
b. 1958
New Orleans

STANLEY
b. 1959
Raleigh, N.C.

Other than showing that Beaulieu men have a way of disappearing, Betty's map of our family was hardly trustworthy. The facts are, my father never talked about his people, and although my parents spoke French and both trapped and fished for a living, my mother always claimed that her father was a businessman from Paris. So if the Beaulieus were Cajun, there'd never be a way of knowing. The way I see it, half the Beaulieus are afraid they're Cajun, and spend their lives pretending to be regular white people, and the other half are afraid they're just regular white people and spend their lives pretending to be Cajun.

No Beaulieu ever felt a duty to tell the truth about anything as important as origins. You can pry lies off a Beaulieu like cloves off a garlic head, and all you'll find at the center is an invisible pocket of stinky air. I have a cousin who recently married a McDermott from Utica, Mississippi, who says she's Irish, and even goes on tours to Ireland where everyone in the group is called McDermott so you only have to learn first names. At the end of the trip, they all get to sit at a big oak table in a bar somewhere and have their pictures taken with a crown on, and told they're Lady or Lord McDermott. My sister Arthurine's spent most of her life in Louisiana, but she once lived in Texas for a year, and ever since she's talked with this Texas debutante drawl. The same year, her husband gave her an ugly pinkish Cadillac, although she did not know how to drive, and she kept the Cadillac parked in front of her house, and sat out there in it, waiting for people to pass by and think she was some kind of society woman. Me, I've done my best to work off my Louisiana accent, and to become one of the from-somewhere-elses of Jersey City: my downstairs neighbor's Egyptian and my landlord's from Chattanooga.

After Betty made herself over in Manny's image, he married her. She worked herself to death as a hospital aide and then a dental receptionist to put him through school. When Netta was born, Betty set up a babysitting ring and charged rich ladies on Audubon Place an arm and a leg to watch after their children and make sure Netta didn't rough them up too much. Betty named her daughter Antoinette—it must have been the Frenchest sounding name she could find, but everyone refused to call the girl anything but Netta.

Manny finally got a degree, and dragged Betty northward to the middle of nowhere where he'd found a job at a little college in Ripon, Wisconsin. For Betty it was worth it. She married for education, she wanted to be somebody. Once, she forced me to go back to high school to get my diploma, to sit with pregnant teenagers in night classes, so I know firsthand the depth of her desperation for personal improvement.

This is why I decided it was a kind of tragedy when I called Betty and learned that Manny had run off with a college dropout half his age, and that Betty was working full-time designing knitwear for a business in Oshkosh, near Ripon, to support herself and her girl. She'd worked as a teacher's assistant for a while, but had to give up the job, because it didn't pay. Nights she studied to become a teacher. She and Netta had moved from their house at the center of town to some isolated place on Ripon's outskirts. I felt bad for Betty, because she hadn't had the sense to marry for money. Manny's salary was so small that suing for alimony wasn't worth the time or the trouble of watching over some snake of a lawyer.

In my day, we looked for a man who could make thirty thousand dollars a year. Because back then, the main thing was not to work. I've been employed as an administrative assistant and a nurse's aide, and I worked for a year or so for this old battle-ax who lived in a big house. There wasn't a part of her body that she didn't have something wrong with it. Get me a knee pad, rub my shoulder here, go down to the drugstore and buy me a cough drop. She was strong as a horse and we both knew it, and I didn't feel bad at all walking out on her. After that, I worked as a teacher's aide and a cook's helper and a wash lady, grocery cashier, babysitter, assistant bookkeeper, and just about anything else, and so I can tell you there isn't a job that's worth your time. If I hadn't had a face so ugly it could stop a truck, I would have done like my sister, Arthurine, and married an old man for his money and lived high until he died ten years later. In Jersey City, Land of Opportunity, I'd found work in the Complaints Office of the Municipal Court, typing up pink summonses to petty criminals, people who had no intention of honoring the invitations. I had taken the job about as far as it could go, and I was glad Betty's letter offered me an excuse to quit.

I gave my landlord notice, and moved all my things into a ten-by-ten-foot storage space. In September, 1974, I got on a Greyhound and rode for twenty-seven hours, until that scented ammonia smell those buses are famous for sank right to my bones. The windows were tinted this dark green on top and you had to slouch down to see the true colors of things. The scenery strung by me dull as old clothes on a wash line: I saw corn rows, blacker and redder in one place than the next, cows here and there like dropped scraps of paper, small look-alike towns, laid-off men loitering on corners with their hands in their pockets. At one depot on the second day, I saw a man push a woman down so hard she couldn't stand up. She sat against a car, moaning and cradling her hips while people circled around her to have a look. A boy in a soldier uniform bent over and whispered a question to her.

Somebody in the crowd said, "God, she's really hurt, somebody take her to the hospital."

"No one's taking her anywhere," said the man who'd done the pushing. "She's my wife."

Then the bus pulled away, and I watched the circle of people until it grew too small to make out.

When I got to Ripon, I could see right off it was an empty sort of place. You pass by a billboard that says: HOME OF SPEED QUEEN WASHING MACHINES, and another that says: YOU ARE ENTERING THE VALLEY OF THE JOLLY GREEN GIANT. There's only three things there: the Speed Queen plant, the canning factory, and the Rippin' Good Cookie company, which makes that pasty kind of cookie you eat when it's the only sweet around. And Ripon's the birthplace of the Republican party. There's nothing there worth knowing about. By the time I arrived, the machines had done their work and cut down all the pig corn. When the bus stopped, I felt like I'd traveled across outer space to find a planet as lifeless as the moon.

The bus let me off outside a variety store, and I didn't see Betty anywhere. I had this terrible feeling I'd gotten off at the wrong state. I went inside the store and asked the saleslady if I was in Ripon. She was a fish-faced type with pale eyes that would remind you of tinfoil. She pretended not to understand what I'd asked. Then she answered as unfriendly and short as she could manage.

"Of course."

Just like that.

"You don't sound like you're from around here," she opened up again, after looking me over. Then her face shut back up, a fish mouth closing on a worm.

"Course *not,*" I answered. There aren't even letters in the alphabet to put down how she and other people I heard later in Ripon talked. Think of Lawrence Welk—they sound like that only ten times worse.

I went back outside. I stood for a while, looking up and down this half strip of street that was plainly the whole town: a five-and-dime, a lone bar called The Spot, a thrift shop, a movie theater, the police station. I leaned against the variety store and the saleslady peered at me, coming up toward the plate glass and backing off again like a pet store minnow.

A white Lincoln Continental pulled up, and out jumped my daughter, Betty, crying "Mama!"

She stepped back so that I could take a look at her. She had on black stretch pants and a yellow beret balanced on her hair like a tiddlywink. She always dressed smart. At that moment, I saw myself: short and broad, wearing an old flowered print that resembled sofa upholstery.

My granddaughter, Netta, didn't get out of the car until Betty and I had hugged and said our hellos. Then Netta shoved open the door and looked out, glaring at my bags and me like an underpaid chauffeur greeting his boss. I hadn't seen Netta for a while, and I was surprised by how little she'd changed. She was small for sixteen, with thick black hair, and a tiny, barely visible mustache that looked like a smudge of car grease.

I gave her a wet grandmother kiss and she sort of brushed my cheek with her lips in return.

I slid into the Lincoln and sat down on a maroon plush seat.

"This is your car?" I asked Betty.

Betty smiled and didn't answer.

"It belongs to Mr. Iodine," Netta said.

"To who?" I asked, but Betty frowned at Netta, so Netta didn't answer. She sat in the front seat and looked at me in the rearview mirror. I stared back and she looked away. She still had Manny's sharp little face and undersized body. But she reminded me of someone else. Me. I had the same black hair cut straight as a knife blade when I was younger, and I'd have that mustache still if I didn't use cream bleach.

I read in magazines on and off about the strong women who are supposed to be around now, raising money and children at the same time, fighting off men at work. Doing all of these things well. Women sort of like James Bond or G.I. Joe, but women. I don't believe in that kind of person. Maybe they're out there in the world, but if I crossed paths with them, they must not have held my attention long enough for me to notice them. The people I've known are more interesting to talk about, full of holes and mistakes.

My daughter and almost all the Beaulieu women except myself just fall apart if life brushes against them wrong. They have to have someone, anyone, around for constant loving and touching. When they lose their men, they feel loneliness to the roots of their hair and the dark centers of their veins. This is why I tried to keep my mouth shut and not be judgmental just because I found out that Betty had coupled up with an army officer fifteen years older than her who was dumb and mean and had a goiter.

You probably don't know what a goiter is. If you grow

up near the ocean, you don't have to. People in landlocked places get them, because they don't eat enough sea fish, and so don't get any iodine. These goiters look like double chins, except that skinny people can have them. And they're leathery instead of soft.

Six weeks after I arrived, a man drove up Union Street to the little house Betty rented on the edge of town. The man had this stretch of skin under his face like a sausage tied at both ends to his ears. I'm sure that some people with goiters carry them well and look fine, but he wasn't one of them. Not that I have anything against ugliness generally. It's just the inequality of it, the way homeliness shapes a woman's life in definite directions, while an ugly man doesn't think twice about snapping up any lady he wants.

Me and Netta were sitting on the bed upstairs, folding laundry, and we watched the man cut across the rectangle of ice in front of the house. Netta says: "There's Mr. Iodine, Mama's beau."

"Her *what*?" I asked.

"That's the man she calls her beau," Netta said. "Her very own Sweet Potato Pie." Then she put her head between her knees and cackled in this diabolical laugh.

So I leaned closer to the window to have a good look: Mr. Iodine was a big, wide man who walked like he had lead shot in his shoes. He was wearing one of those olive green parkas lined with orange nylon inside and rimmed on the hood with something that looks like cat fur. Everyone up there uses them. A military uniform jabbed out the bottom of his coat. His hood was down, so I could see the Kennedy half dollar bald spot in the middle of his silver hair.

"What's that thing on his neck?" I asked my granddaughter.

"A goiter," Netta told me. "It's from not having enough sense to eat iodized salt." I took a good look before Mr. Iodine tripped on a piece of ice and slid around to the door.

We heard Betty answer the doorbell, and from then on, we listened to her voice chattering up through the floorboards. Every now and then, Mr. Iodine's laugh would shake the floor.

"He's from Oshkosh," said Netta, twisting a red sock and a black one together. I picked up the socks as soon as she put them down, and I balled them up with their matches. Netta's mouth twisted into a smile under her mustache. She looked like a villain in one of those silent movies.

"He's a high-ranking officer in the Green Beret. He's usually away on secret missions." When Netta said this, she dropped her voice and raised her eyebrows like she might be imitating the way he talked about himself. "What he does is *top secret*. He can't even tell Mama where he goes." She leaned closer to me and whispered, "But me and my friend Barb figured it out anyway. Every time he leaves on one of his trips, there's something in the news about people being killed in Asia or Africa or someplace. He probably tortures people for the U.S. government."

"Netta!" I said in a shocked grandmother voice. "Don't pull my leg."

The chattering below dimmed to a murmur. Then we hear, "Hey you two!" Betty's voice knocked on the floor, like she knew what we were talking about. "Come down here and say hi."

I got right up because I wanted to meet this Mr. Iodine.

Netta groaned and stayed where she was, until Betty stuck her head in the door and said, "Won't you join us too, hun?" The way Betty can ask for something melts your heart like butter. Netta made a face, but came with me downstairs.

I watched my daughter's hips swish in front of me. Betty is a real Beaulieu. She has pretty reddish hair although she frosts it to make it look strawberry blond. She's small with thin ankles and wrists and she has little freckles all over her, delicate like the spots on a tiger lily. When I followed her down the stairs into the kitchen, I couldn't help but be impressed.

She turned to me and said, "His name is Mr. Buster Dodge. You go right in the TV room, Mama. I'm going to get his dinner going."

" 'Lo," he said when Netta and I sat down across from him on the couch. It's like that up there, people don't get uncomfortable if they just sit and stare and say almost nothing.

Then I found myself creeping up on me in a way you wouldn't have liked to see. I all of a sudden got this nice smile and started flirting with him. My daughter's own sweetheart. I couldn't stop myself. I was a silly sight with my big ugly face mooning up at him.

"So you're a Green Beret," I said. "What kind of things do you do?"

"Heh-hem," Mr. Iodine said, clearing his throat to work his way up to a sentence. "Just stuff. Nothing a lady would care about."

"That's a handsome shirt," I went on. It was the only thing he was wearing that didn't have an army look to it—a blue plaid flannel. "Did you get it around here?"

"Got it off a dead nigger," he told me.

Netta smirked and said, "There's about four hundred John Birch Societies right here in this one county."

I looked at Mr. Iodine to see if he was insulted, but he didn't seem to understand that she was tormenting him. He was staring at her legs. When he saw I was watching him, he got off the couch and walked to the kitchen.

"Betty!" he called. "Where's the Blatz? I thought you were going to pick up a case of Blatz."

"There's beer in your car. I'll get it in a minute," Betty answered.

Mr. Iodine cleared his throat again, loud and forceful, in a way I noted might get on your nerves if he did this a lot, and then he walked over to Betty's television and turned it on.

"She's lonely," I whispered to Netta.

"Who isn't?" said my granddaughter.

I watched two lines of fat, broad-shouldered boys crawling out of a ditch somewhere in Europe. They had helmets with plastic leaves glued to them, and all around the earth flowered orange and gray from grenades. I've always noticed how some men who have been in a world war can't stop watching war movies. It gives me the creeps, because I imagine myself having been somewhere with a bunch of women friends, say in a department store. All of a sudden bombs are falling and bullets are flying and then there's funerals for all the women where they get tucked into red and blue flags and a cannon goes off. Then I ask myself, if that happened to my friends, would I want to spend the rest of my life watching movies of women being killed by grenades in department stores?

I sure as hell wouldn't.

Netta abandoned me in the living room and I could hear her thumping down plates on the kitchen table while Betty rattled around the stove. "I'll go try and find that beer," I called into the kitchen.

When I walked out the front door, the cold surprised me so bad I stopped breathing. It was only October, but the wind stabbed at me from all directions like a hundred knives. I went back inside and got an old coat of Betty's, some mittens, a hat, and a scarf. When I opened the door a second time, my feet turned instantly to ice. They walked without feeling, crunching the dead grasses under the snow.

Mr. Iodine's Lincoln Continental had a pelt of snow-flakes on it, and I had to fight with the car door, which was stuck with the cold. I reached for a case of Blatz beer. Next to it were yellow and blue buckets, two hunting knives, some bullets and shotgun shells, a rifle lying half outside its leather jacket against the car seat, and a bright orange vest.

Inside the yellow bucket were a skinned rabbit and a trap with a rabbit foot still in it. The animal must have tried to pull its leg off and run. Mr. Iodine had made a mess of the skinning. I could see little pieces of meat stuck to the inside of the rabbit hide, where he had failed to scrape it. My mother used to skin a rabbit so clean it was like rolling a silk stocking off your leg, so I knew a bad job when I'd seen one.

In the blue bucket I found a second trap with a rabbit in it, but this one was still alive. Its eyes were glazed and its legs still, but its heart pumped beneath the fur, and clean blood trickled through the teeth of the trap, where they clamped one leg. It made me sick with pity. I looked behind me through the house window. Mr. Iodine was sitting at the table, while Betty scurried back and forth putting down plates and bowls.

I picked up one of the knives and killed the rabbit. I removed it from the trap, and opened the car door facing away from the house for some light. There in the cold I pulled off my mittens, set the rabbit down on the snow, and cut through the neck, slit the belly, took out the bowels, and turned the skin from the meat. I pulled the rabbit's paws from its fur gloves as gently as you'd pull a baby's feet out of its pajamas. This was something I hadn't done in forty years, and I watched my hands move like they were a little girl's, agile and quick and sure despite the cold. I wiped my hands in the snow and pulled my mittens back on. I opened the car door wide for more light and scraped the hide, put the tiny pieces of meat in the bucket, and stretched the skin over the bucket's rim. Then I picked up the case of beer, slammed the car door with my foot, and went back into the house.

At dinner, I got to liking my daughter's boyfriend less and less. First, Betty served a fancy meal he hardly noticed: real steak, which Netta heaped with iodized salt, turnip greens cooked with just the right amount of bacon fat, potatoes, and deep-dish apple Betty with whipped cream.

"Tomorrow I'm cooking Spanish," Betty announced after she sat down. "I got a recipe for codfish stew from a teacher in my class."

"*Cod*fish? We don't eat that crap in Wisconsin," Mr. Iodine said. "We send it out east where the Jews will pay twenty dollars a pound for it." He snickered over his steak. "No fish for me, thank you."

Then he started what may be the dumbest conversation

I've ever heard. He says: "See this strip of fat on the beef? That happens when they fatten the animals in the slaughterhouse at the last minute. The meat doesn't have a chance to get marbled, so it isn't tasty. Now in *Chile*"—he lowered his voice as if the fact he'd been there might be top secret—"they have range-fed beef. You don't find good beef like that here anymore."

So Netta tells him: "In New Mexico, they just let the cows and steers walk up and down the land, they don't fence them in. You got to build a fence around your yard to keep them out. They have these white floppy-ear cows, Charolais and a few Herefords here and there. You can just be walking along and bump into them. Then in Louisiana, you got the Brahma cattle along the coast who roam around in these marshy pastures you can't see the end of, they're so big. They keep Brahmas down there because their feet can stand the wet without rotting."

Mr. Iodine looked at her like he was giving out army commands and a recruit had interrupted him. I wondered where Netta had gotten her information, and thought maybe she had read it in *National Geographic*. Her speech must have exhausted everything she knew about cattle.

Mr. Iodine asked, "Cows? Did you say cows? I never heard of a Hereford *cow* before."

Now no one at the table could figure what he was getting at. Not even Betty, who was shoveling more greens onto Mr. Iodine's plate, and giving him an I-aim-to-please smile.

"They must have been steers," he said, sneering at Netta.

"Down the road, there's some lady Herefords with their calves, and a big bull," Netta told him.

"That's wrong," said Mr. Iodine. "Because there's no such thing as a female Hereford. There's female milk cows like Guernseys. There are Hereford steers and Hereford bulls, and that's all."

My mouth sort of dropped open, and I managed to say, "Hereford is a breed, like Angus."

"I've never seen an Angus cow either. Have *you* ever seen an Angus cow?"

Well I laughed, thinking he was just teasing us, but he was dead serious. Because he didn't stop there. He carried on and the same sentences about Herefords and Angus kept repeating themselves. He was one of those stupid people who make a point that way.

Finally, he stood up to get his third Blatz. Netta leans to me across the table and says, "You cut them in half and they grow into two bulls like earthworms." She fell out laughing. I saw Betty's eye fixed on me, and tried hard to hold myself in, but a laugh sort of sputtered through me, like water pushes through someone's hand clamped over a faucet.

"Mr. Dodge is one of the highest ranking officers in the Green Beret," says my daughter. "He went to an Ivy League school called Dartmouth."

Netta was holding her sides as if she might burst. She ran upstairs to the bathroom and slammed the door. I could hear her laughing, loud as rain on a metal roof.

I made amends as best I could. I shooed Betty out of the kitchen and told her to snuggle up with Buster on the couch and watch TV. She went upstairs and changed into a nightie made of some kind of lavender gauze, and matching slippers, and sat down next to her sweetheart. Betty lifted his arm and placed it around her shoulders so he'd hug her.

At the commercial, he came into the kitchen to mix some drinks he called napalm bomberoos. Vodka with lime and V-8 juice and a little hot pepper. He made a huge strong one for himself and a little weak one for her. I ignored him because I was scrubbing like mad at the pans Betty had left in the oven. She's a good cook, but when she's done making a meal, the kitchen looks like a war zone. She dirties three times as many pans as you could imagine a use for, leaving all of them black and crusty on the bottom. Plates were strewn on little piles of silverware, dirty napkins, onion skins and garlic and everything else. After forty minutes I wasn't near done cleaning.

Betty and Mr. Iodine turned on a vampire movie and all these creepy sounds started coming from the TV room. I wanted to get out of that kitchen quick, because things like that scare me. I've never been afraid of men when I'm walking alone in the city through the dark night. I always figure I could pick up a broken bottle and throw it at them, or fend them off with a stick. But something that comes at you while you're asleep and sucks your blood so that before you know it you're done for and one of them, that's scary. There you are lying all shut-eyed and defenseless.

A lady screamed in the next room. I pulled up my shirt collar and tried not to listen to the organ music from the TV. I banged the pans louder than I needed until I finished the last one. When I walked into the front room to say good night to Betty, she had already turned in and gone upstairs. Mr. Iodine was asleep on the couch, his hair tickling the empty bomberoo glasses. He smelled dead drunk. I shut off the TV, keeping my eyes on the far wall, and went upstairs.

Netta and I had single beds right next to each other,

Netta's by the door and mine by the window. She looked asleep. I undressed in the dark for fear she was really awake and would see parts of my body I like to keep hidden. Like my big stomach and sacks-of-meal breasts. Even young, I was not much to look at. I've been ugly so long I've grown accustomed to it. Still, I don't show the things I love to those who can't be expected to admire them. Netta as I said was no great beauty, but it's a long way between her jackrabbit body and the thing I wear now, and it might have been a shock to my granddaughter to see what the distance could do even to her.

I put on wool socks and a flannel nightgown and slipped between my sheets, which were cold as coffin lids. I tossed around to warm up the bed. After a long time, I fell asleep.

A cry slipped through my heart like a bayonet, and I awoke.

I sat up and made out the outline of a big man, wrapped in darkness. My heart leapt. I pushed above the waters of sleep and saw more clearly: Mr. Iodine. I could smell the napalm bomberoos on his breath, and he was pushing himself up from where he'd fallen widthways across Netta's bed.

"Oh gimme some, Betty, I haven't gotten enough since 'Nam," he told Netta. He sank to his knees, put his head on Netta's bed and pulled on her covers.

"Get off me, you dumb fuck!" Netta yelled, pinned under the blankets.

I was already tugging at him. I dragged him upward with all my strength, which can be mighty at times. I banged him against the wall and shook him until his teeth rattled. I pushed him in the direction of the staircase and he stumbled down, miraculously not falling. I saw Betty's bedroom door open but I didn't stop; I followed Mr. Iodine down the stairs and pushed him to the front door. I took his coat from the closet and heaved it at him. His car keys fell out and I stuck them back in his pocket. And while he stood there clutching the coat like it might hold him up, I opened the door and shoved him into the bitter cold.

Upstairs, I stepped back through our bedroom door and ran into Betty. She was saying over and over to Netta, "What happened? Why's Mama throwing him out?"

The light from the hall showed Netta frowning at Betty, sternly, as a mother might look at a daughter.

"He thought he was in your room," I explained. "He was so drunk he came in and fell on Netta's bed, so I put him out."

Now Betty glared at me. "You put him out in the cold?" She ran to the window. Over her shoulder, I could see Mr. Iodine's car lights moving down the road in a red bric-a-brac pattern.

"How could you do that?" Betty yelled, turning on me. "What if he doesn't come back or has an accident? You've been drunk yourself!" She ran into her bedroom and slammed the door.

"So I have!" I called after her. "But I never half-killed a person I thought was someone else by falling on them in the late night!"

I got back into bed and heard Betty crying in her room.

"It's OK," my granddaughter consoled me. "I would have killed him anyway if you hadn't thrown him out." I heard her turn away from me under her comforter.

I had bad, confusing dreams. In the morning, while I was fighting to open my eyes, I sank back asleep and dreamed a blue-eyed wolf was gnawing on my neck bone. The wolf reminded me of my father and youngest brother, because both had liked neck bones, fighting over them and sucking them noisily at Thanksgiving. The wolf sent tooth-shaped flashes of pain up my spine and into the back of my head.

When I finally opened one eye, the moon looked like an aspirin tablet behind the bluish window glass. I moved slightly and the pain in my neck bit clean through me. I turned my head slowly to test exactly how much trouble my back was going to give me after lifting a two-hundred-pound bag of man the night before. I decided I could keep the pain under control by slow movement. I sat up and I realized it was not the moon, but the Wisconsin sun, struggling to burn through the clouds. And there in the field behind the house was Netta, throwing snowballs at the snow. I knew I had to talk woman-to-girl to her.

As I sat, the pain clawed itself upward into my hair, and when I stood, it crawled downward, circling between my shoulder blades. It took me forever to dress, what with the long winter underwear and all the socks, but I finally rose, fully clothed, and went down the stairs one at a time. I crept across the snow behind my granddaughter. Even inside her parka, she looked slight, narrow-shouldered. The field of snow stretched before her, enormous, midwestern. "Netta, let's talk," I called out to her.

Netta threw a snowball at a hump of ice and kept her back to me. "Mind your own business, you fat old sow," she answered.

What I thought at this point was how that girl didn't have any sense of place. Here she was in a town she hardly knew, where people barely talked, an outsider looking in. She didn't have the benefit of a home like Jersey City, where people belong because almost everyone's from somewhere else. Netta's place was Betty, the only thing she had always been near. And then I thought of the Beaulieus in general: they're like a bowl of sour ball candies knocked from your hand, scattering away in every direction. The girls have fled to Wisconsin, North Carolina, Little Rock, San Diego. And of course the men are heaven knows where, wherever men go. I sometimes think there might be an island way far off, where traveling salesmen and long-gone fathers and sailors meet, a kind of big place with tables and uniforms, like an Elks Club in which they all sit around acting buddy-buddy. But the truth is, everyone seems shiftless, in constant motion. No one has any sense of beginning or destination anymore.

"Netta, don't be too mad at your mother. We Beaulieus got to stick together. I know it's hard for you here," I started.

She threw a new snowball, and then nine more at the hole made by the first one, and I watched respectfully. They each rose steadily in perfect arcs, and hit dead center. When she was done, the hole she had made in the ice was the size of a single snowball.

"Mama's just staring into her coffee looking lost," Netta told me without turning around. "Why don't you go inside and fix her some pancakes and cheer her up?"

I left my granddaughter there and took her advice. A bite of pain sunk between my shoulder blades with every little thing I did that morning—reaching for the flour, mixing the batter, lighting the stove under the skillet, heaping the pancakes onto Betty's plate although she refused to eat them.

* * *

Mr. Iodine was still not to be seen after three weeks. I'd watch the news, and sure enough, there were reports all over the world about countries being invaded and wars going on, and I couldn't help thinking he might be involved in all those evilish things at the same time.

Betty wanted him back despite everything. She got quieter and sadder every day. This was a fact that stabbed me like a broken rib every time I breathed. It was hard to deal with the understanding that my own daughter was so fragile.

I should confess that I saw how unfairly Betty's weakness was a product of my own strength, which led me to do a terrible thing when Betty was young. You see, when I was sixteen, I ran off to Franklin, Louisiana, with Betty's father, a boy named Dorian Daigle. We never married, but he stayed with me for ten years after Betty was born, and we held ourselves out as married. Franklin was that kind of small place where everyone knew more about you than you did about yourself, where town opinion was as deadly and inescapable as malaria. You will understand then why, when Dorian abandoned us, I pretended to have murdered him. That was back when I still cared what people thought, and the public shame of having been deserted by your loving husband was not something that I cared to deal with each and every day of my life. The embarrassment of having murdered him was nothing, in comparison.

Three days after Dorian left, I got a big gunnysack and stuffed it with his clothes and Spanish moss until it was the size and shape of a body. Then I dragged it out the back door, right past the window of my nosy next-door neighbor, this old witch named Lotta Plum. I loaded the bag in a wheelbarrow, pushed it down the road, and dumped it into Bayou Teche.

This led to more trouble than you could believe even now. That Lotta Plum called the sheriff. Once I was arrested, how could I prove Dorian was alive when I had no idea where he was? They dragged the Teche for his body, and then they kept me in jail three years, waiting for enough evidence to convict me. If this story seems improbable to you, you just don't know enough about the law, the terrible snarls of its diabolical lace, the gaudy complexity of its injustices.

It took Dorian showing up in person at the courthouse when he finally got wind of the problem, for them to let me out. He had followed the oil industry to Port Arthur and then Tampico, and was working as a driller and living with a woman named Jewel, who knew a man who knew a girl who knew Lotta Plum and that was how Dorian finally learned that I'd killed him.

Even after Dorian came all the way home to set things straight, the authorities were suspicious that he was only impersonating himself, that he was an imposter come to force life into a dead man. "Christ in hell," he told the old idiot who was chief judge at the time, "do I have to die to convince you that I'm the murdered Dorian Daigle?"

As soon as they let me out, Dorian evaporated like a ghost. I went to collect my daughter. I had sent Betty to live with my newly widowed sister, Arthurine, in New Orleans, and she had taught Betty to be delicate and pretentious. When I arrived to retrieve her, Betty clung to Arthurine, and told me she wanted to stay in New Orleans with her and Arthurine's daughter, Gert, a girl without a scrap of fierceness to her.

After I agreed to move in with them, I learned that Betty liked Gert because Betty could show her up by acting perfect and dressing perfect and dating the right boys and helping out Arthurine. In a way, Betty stole Gert from Arthurine, because Gert changed into someone else from having Betty around—she sassed her mother and went out with wild boys and finally married a man just because Arthurine and Betty disapproved of him. It is one of the ironies of fate that, years later, Arthurine's grandson would end up in trouble with the law and she would beg me to take him in and help raise him.

Betty stole herself from me, too. For months after they freed me, Betty pretended I was not her real mother, but just an interloper. She once even introduced me to her school friends as a next-door neighbor. She was so full of pretensions I wondered if I would be able to recognize her if she ever finally showed her true self.

After Mr. Iodine left, Betty floated around the house, haunting it with her empty looks. She blamed me that Buster Dodge hadn't stayed with her every possible moment he was back in Wisconsin. It wasn't fair of her to act that way, but she couldn't help it. Between watching her pine like that, and watching the world outside the house growing uglier with cold every day, I got the closest to desolate I've ever felt in my life.

All November I sat by myself in the house during the day, and watched Lawrence Welk, sewed new curtains, knitted a knee-length sweater, and generally did the cooking and washing. I was deadly bored. I didn't ever meet anybody from Ripon, except for occasional introductions to Netta's friends. Nobody my age. Only once, this old busybody stopped by in the town Book Mobile—a squat lady with a feathery layered hairdo that looked like a rooster had sat on her head and died there. She stood at the door, asking prying questions about Betty and Mr. Iodine and trying to wheedle her way inside. She was still talking when I closed the door.

The house Betty rented was one of those prefabricated aluminum-sided things. There were two other new ones on the road, but they were still unoccupied. The nearest lived-in house was a mile up the hill, and the nearest building was the National Rifle Association, about one-half mile away. Everything else was empty fields, except for a place called Kiwanis Park across the gravel road. And that really wasn't even a park, it was just a little valley with yellow grass sticking through the snow in the fall.

One day I got so lonesome I was past standing it. Betty had told me she was coming home late, and Netta was going to eat dinner at her friend Barb's place. I couldn't bear the thought of sitting by myself in that aluminum house for so many hours. I found a parka at the back of the closet and put it on—it was brown and heavy and might have belonged to Manny once. As I zipped it up, I pretended that wherever he was at that moment, he would suddenly feel occupied by an uncomfortable presence.

I crossed the gravel road to walk in Kiwanis. It was a sad place, with gray woods bordering on one side, the gray sky hovering over it, and a little gray shack in a sunken area in the side of a hill. I made my way toward the shack since there was nothing else in sight worth going to. It was only four o'clock, but the twilight was already creeping up everywhere. I had such a strong feeling of homesickness, thinking how anyplace else in the world would seem more like a home than Ripon.

Inside the shack were a mattress, a few beer bottles, condoms flung onto the floor, and big pieces of chipped paint. I walked up a little stairway and on the second floor found another mattress, all surrounded by the same kind of litter. I sat down on the mattress and looked out into Kiwanis Park.

Even shielded from the wind, after ten minutes, I was already freezing. But I stayed there. I'd been feeling cold for so long I hardly cared anymore. Pretty soon I saw Netta and Barb coming down the path. Barb was more grown-up than Netta. I knew she had quit high school early and was living by herself in the bottom part of a house in the center of town. I could see her makeup from forty feet away, and she had on a hot pink parka. I pressed my eye to the knothole and spied on them, just to have something to do.

Then I saw they were heading for the shack. All of a sudden I was terrified. I thought, they'll think I'm crazy if they find me, a grandmother, sitting up here by myself in this old place. I considered going down the stairs and walking out like it was the most natural thing in the world for me to be there, and they could mind their own business. But by the time I stood up and stepped over the mattress, I could hear them entering below. I sidled away from the stairway.

"Man, look at these rubbers all over the floor," I heard Barb say. "Imagine doing it on this mattress!"

"There's another one upstairs," Netta answered. Then she added, "Once Mr. Iodine came up here with his pistol and shot at the crab apples my mother tossed up into the air for him."

Barb snickered. "I saw him down at The Spot a few days ago, trying to get them to make him a napalm bomb-eroo."

"You saw him here? I thought he was still away on one of his secret missions. You know whenever he's about to disappear, he comes over and watches TV and gets drunk on Blatz. Then he gets mad and storms out and doesn't come back until after his trip, so my mother worries about him."

I hadn't exactly realized all this was something he did regular.

"Bob Biedenharn knocked up Laura Senkowski on this mattress and then her father threw her out," Barb said.

"I wish you'd been there for Mr. Iodine's visit this time. Before he left, he got so drunk he came into my room and fell down on my bed."

"Oh haw haw!" says Barb. "He just wanted you to kiss his pretty face!"

Netta laughed. "You should have seen my grandmother. She jumped out of her bed and started screeching at him. It was *fun*ny. She pounded on his big ugly back and his eyes got enormous. He was scared to death. He lit outta there. I thought she was going to pull off his goiter."

I couldn't help it, I had to laugh too. It was one of those big belting laughs brought on by low jokes. As soon as I'd done it, I was sorry. Of course the girls heard me.

Barb came up the stairs, gawked at me, and said, "What the fuck? Hey, it's your grandmother."

All my years didn't tell me how to handle this situation. So I just stood still, and let them handle it until I saw they weren't going to at all.

"I was up here wondering," I explained, "if maybe we could make Betty a birthday cake and have a little party for her, to get her spirits up. Betty told me she's taking a half day off for her birthday, so maybe I could make the cake at Barb's house so Betty doesn't catch on." I didn't think of this until it luckily flew out of my mouth.

"Well sure," said Barb. "That's fine."

Then we all stood around feeling uncomfortable.

"We could go to dinner at Moxie's outside town," said Netta.

I knew that Barb and Netta would expect me to pay, but I was thankful and relieved, although I held in my feelings the way the cold warps you into doing. "OK," I said. "My treat." I followed behind the girls up the slope of the park, stepping into their footprints to keep as much snow as possible out of my boots.

Moxie's is a dark, warm place that offers liquor and a hot meal. The eating area is a murky brown sea with white tablecloths glimmering in the dark recesses like oyster shells under water. The girls ordered muskie, and I had walleye, and when we got in Barb's Mustang to drive home, you could smell the wild fresh fish on our breaths. I closed my eyes and pretended to myself I was near the ocean. The Mustang had chains on but slid and skidded around corners. Barb drove about a hundred miles an hour along back roads to the house. I was sorry when the car pulled up Union Street.

Barb let us off at the bottom of our road because she was afraid her car would get stuck in a snowbank on the incline. When Netta and me stepped out of the Mustang, the cold almost knocked us down like a big dog. We bent forwards and wrapped our scarves tight but the wind still gnawed through them.

As we walked up the hill, the white Lincoln Continental turned the other bend sharply and sped like a getaway car from the house. I could see my daughter through the front window, slumped on the couch. The Lincoln jumped onto the highway and tore up the hill in that bric-a-brac pattern.

"Look who's been here!" The wind snatched Netta's voice away from me.

We knocked our boots on the steps and as soon as I went in, I could see Betty drunk out of her mind, curled up on the couch and clutching an empty vodka bottle as tight as she might a man's arm. I was sorry that Netta had to see this. All us older Beaulieus drink like fish, but we can hold it. I walked over to the couch and touched Betty on the shoulder.

"What's wrong with me?" she moaned at us. "How come nobody loves me the way I do him? Buster's been here for ten days and he only came to see me now, the night before he's going away again. He doesn't even have anywhere to stay but a cold hotel."

"Don't be a stupid fool," I told my daughter. "*I* love you the way you do him." Netta and me pulled Betty up gently and walked her upstairs to her bedroom. Netta turned down the covers while I undressed my daughter and put a nightgown on her. We tucked her in.

The snow fell all night and the next day, so that on my daughter's birthday the drifts were midway up the telephone poles. Netta got up early to dig a tunnel from the front door to the gravel road. Betty had already left for work. Barb came to the bottom of the road to pick us up. I carried a grocery bag of ingredients to the car and Barb drove me to her house so I could make Betty's birthday cake in secret. The girls told me they'd pick me and the cake up after Netta got out of school. Netta did not look as if she planned to stop by the school. She was in a pretty cheerful mood.

I slaved over that cake. There were three layers, cooked one at a time because Barb's kitchen only had one cake pan. I made chiffon cake batter and blended half of it with green food dye and the other with red dye and cherry jam, so when I put the layers together it was striped in Christmas colors. I mixed pure butter and sugar white icing, and decorated it with green and red cherries. I colored half the leftover icing pink and half green, and made three wax paper decorators, two with slits at the end for roses and leaves and two more with plain openings to write "Happy Birthday, Be Happy Betty Beaulieu" in green and "37" in pink.

You've never seen such a cake. It was a pure effort of mother love. I took from early morning until one o'clock to cook all the layers and let them cool, then ice and decorate them. When I finished, I set the cake on the kitchen table and admired it and waited for the girls to come home and admire it too.

I waited an hour and Barb and Netta didn't show. I found out later that they had gone ice fishing all morning at Green Lake, and then headed back in plenty of time, around one o'clock, to get me. Only Barb's Mustang skidded them into a snowbank and held them up for hours. But I wasn't thinking about reasons.

I've always been bad at waiting for things. By 3:30 I was really stewing. Leave it to them to forget all about me, I thought. I wanted to get back just an hour or so after Betty came home from her half day. I didn't want her to sit long all alone in that empty house on her birthday.

But I wasn't eager to go home on foot either. The

quickest way there from Barb's house was to walk to the end of a dead-end road and then turn down a path through Kiwanis Park. It was all maybe less than a mile walk and I might be able to do it in forty minutes going slowly over the icy patches, but forty minutes in that cold will freeze your face right off your head.

So I waited another hour and the girls didn't come. By then I was steaming with anger, too mad to think about the cold. I ransacked Barb's cupboards and found a big casserole dish that just fit upside down over the cake plate, so I could keep the icing from getting mussed up. Then I put on my boots, coat, gloves, mittens, hat, and scarf and walked through the mountains of snow to the dead end.

My breath made smoky coils in front of me and my lungs ached with the cold. There was ice everywhere and when I stepped onto the path that slopes from the road to the edge of the park I lost my balance. I spun around on my left ankle and all I could think of was that I was going to drop that cake. I lifted my hands over my head so that the cake would be the last thing to hit the ground and I fell forward into a snowdrift. My elbows jabbed into the drift's crust and it splintered in my face and little pieces of ice fell between my neck and the collar of my coat. But the cake was safe, resting right on the crust above my elbows, the casserole dish still in place.

I picked myself up and brushed the snow off the front of my clothes. I lifted the plate and casserole dish gently and peeked inside and saw the cake was in good condition. I made my way slowly down the hill and past the shack. The splintered ice slipped inside the front of my shirt and the wind bit my ears through my hat. By the time I got to the bottom of the hill I was crying with the cold. My toes felt like stones in my boots. I inched along in a straight line, careful for the cake. I kept my face down so the wind wouldn't hit it full on and I only glanced up every now and then to make sure I was going in the right direction. That's why I didn't see Mr. Iodine until I tripped over him.

He was lying on his side on top of the snow, stiff as a tin soldier. My toe caught on the hood of his jacket and I fell headlong into a drift. The casserole dish jumped away from me into the snow, then turned sideways and tossed out the cake. It tumbled over and the cherries rolled off it in a little line. The cake slid about five feet on its face, leaving behind pink and green tracks.

I pulled myself up and took a good look at Mr. Iodine—I saw the vodka bottle snuggled up against him, and his pale blue nose poking from under the cat fur hood. I unzipped his parka, held my ear to his heart, and zipped him back up. Then I walked as fast as I could up the hill out of the park, and crept into the house without making any noise. I heard Betty in her room upstairs, so I called the hospital from the downstairs phone. By the time I got the courage to tell Betty, the ambulance was already parked on the edge of the gravel road. Betty watched the men roll the frozen body onto a stretcher, and insisted on riding in the ambulance.

I stayed in Ripon a full year, from harvest to harvest, but mostly what I remember are the cold, dead-white days. I tried to get Betty to come and live with me in Jersey City, but she refused. She was almost done with studying to be a teacher, and she told me she wanted to stay and make something of herself.

One night toward the end of August, I couldn't sleep. The moon over the field looked like a white rock embedded in mud. The air had a dirty smell, not like Louisiana. Most of my early life, I could smell the Gulf of Mexico from wherever I stood. If I just breathed in deep enough I could count on that familiar salt taste filling my mouth. I could feel the air stir through me and think, This air's traveled all over, it's twirled over the gulf in hurricanes and blown across far-off islands. September in Jersey City would be like that: you could look at a crowd and think, They've been everywhere, Santo Domingo and the Philippines, Russia and Brazil, they've crossed oceans and clouds and mountains to get here. I couldn't feel that way in my daughter's house. Around me was a sea of earth, dead still. I knew it was time to go back home and live for a while. Not work hard, or try at mothering, or anything so strenuous.

PIGGLY WIGGLY

"OH NETTA, he's such a big beautiful illusion of a man!" Daisy Shekailo warned me. She leaned forward on my mother's couch, balancing an empty can of Blatz beer on the armrest. "I used to think he treated me nice. But when he dragged me to this Wisconsin hellhole, everything changed. Whenever I told him I didn't want to mind his boys, he'd say, 'That's really beneath you, Day, I can't believe you talking about two little kids that way, Day,' and I'd say, 'I just want a little time alone with you, just to pretend that I'm at the center of somebody's world the way you're at the center of mine.' It took me so long to realize he just wanted his own free at no cost slave babysitter." Daisy creased the Blatz can and bent it double. "I feel sorry for that girl, whoever she is!

"When I met him, I thought he was so wonderful, such a responsible father to his kids—*responsible* isn't the word, he didn't have a penny in his pocket for us after he paid his wife maintenance. And those goddamn pigs! I thought I'd lose my mind watching them, I'd find myself thinking, God if they'd just wander on the road and get hit by cars, so we could pack up and move to the city and get out of god-awful Ripon."

She settled the beer can on the floor and looked at me defiantly. "I swear I'd kill that girl if I knew who she was! Who is she to weasel in on us so soon after we separated? Christ, these local girls don't learn jackshit about contraception, how do I know she isn't pregnant?

"I want him back! All I feel is this terrible loss, this emptiness, right here, over my thighs, right smack in the center of me, this emptiness that goes on and on, big as life. Don't ever do what I did! Don't ever promise not to have children just for some man! Because you know what I want now more than anything is real children, my children. I want one named Sherry and another one who's tall like my father. And I'm never going to have any of that! How am I supposed to start over at the age of thirty-eight?" She threw her beer can at the wall, and ran out of the house, banging the screen door.

I stayed in my mother's favorite armchair, looking at the beer trickle down the wall, wondering whether I had enough savings to leave Ripon there and then, and whether I could risk finishing my last weeks of work at the Shekailo place, because, you see, I was that girl, the one Daisy felt so sorry for and the one she wanted to kill.

• • •

If anything that summer had happened differently, I might not have left town in September on my mother's advice.

But I was nineteen and looking for something that would kick the world as I knew it out from under me. I had only one definite plan in life. I was never going to fall in love with a local boy and settle down in the hellhole of Ripon, Wisconsin. I would get out—probably I would head to Jersey City, where my cousin, Stanley, had moved after he got in trouble with the law in Louisiana. His mother had sent him to stay with my grandmother, who had a new job working as a bailiff in the Jersey City criminal court. My grandmother was funny and ugly and independent, and except for the ugly, I wanted to be like her. Not like my mother, whose whole life was a journey from one man to the next after my father left her for a girl half his age.

My mother was in Minneapolis for the summer taking education courses at the university and scouting around for out-of-state husband material. And expecting me, she said, to keep up the house, earn some money, and behave. I had worked for three years part-time at the Piggly Wiggly, since my father stopped sending child support, and now I was putting in fifty hours a week. I was saving up to go to college or to buy a Silverado truck, I hadn't decided which.

The air in the Piggly Wiggly was stale and thin, trapped by double sets of electric doors and held over from winter. There, Ripon collected and fermented in the gossip at the cash registers. You have to think of the Piggly Wiggly as a kind of information clearinghouse—the town only had one grocery store, and everyone passed through its check-out counters at one time or another. So working at the Piggly Wiggly, I got to be kind of omniscient.

I should warn you that town rumors there are dangerous: insidious as poisonous gases, surprising as rattlesnakes, swift as semi trucks gone out of control down a mountain. On the first day of high school, the teachers will already be exchanging gossip about your family at the lunch tables in the teachers' room. Riponite bank tellers and store owners will eye you suspiciously. People you've never met will shoo their children away from you, or approach you for easy sex or marijuana or stare at you angrily from a soda counter. If you live in Ripon, there are always two of you: the person you really are, and the rumor-image of you that everyone else sees, that has nothing to do with you and does not resemble you in any way, but which will always shield you from being known and understood.

I should warn you also that the town will resent my telling you about Ripon—the viciousness of its winters, its hatred of liveliness, its bottomless devouring snows. People there will tell you that I, a troublemaker whose stay in Ripon was short and bent on escape, can only talk about the town out of a presumptuous arrogance. That even now, I view Ripon without accuracy or sensitivity. Nevertheless, this story is purely factual. Where not based on direct participation and observation, it relies on my indifferent gathering of empirical evidence in Piggly Wiggly's aisles.

It was at the Piggly Wiggly, when I was fourteen and before I began working there, that I was first exposed to Mrs. Wallington, a daily customer and town gossip of extraordinary and prophetic powers. I pushed my shopping cart toward the cold cuts section, where Mrs. Wallington stood talking with Mrs. Bozeman, the variety store's clerk.

"When you think," Mrs. Wallington said, "how her

parents did without to send her to the college, just to have her drop out to start selling tie-dyed shirts."

"Is that so?" Mrs. Bozeman answered, looking slightly bored and pretending not to listen, the way she did when she sorted through the thread at the variety store. With a scientific attention to detail, she compared different brands of bratwurst.

"She certainly couldn't return to school once she started carrying on with that professor with the mustache."

"I guess not."

"He should be throttled," Mrs. Wallington continued. "Ruining a young girl's life like that. And from what I hear, she's not the first: he'll fornicate with anything that isn't nailed down. I pity his family, that's what."

I knew so little about my own life at this time, that I did not even imagine she was talking about us.

My father had dragged us to Ripon from New Orleans, in July 1972, a year before I started high school. He'd invited my cousin, Stanley, to stay with us for the summer, saying that the country air would have a salutary effect on him. As things turned out, it didn't—Ripon affected me and Stanley the same way. It filled us with that longing that makes you want to shoot out windows, to drive at breakneck speed through roadblocks, to flee wherever you are. By the end of the summer, Stanley had broken so many laws, my mother had to send him back to his family in New Orleans, where the lawlessness he acquired in Ripon would only dog him.

When my father drove us past the sign at the town limit that said, "POPULATION 7,210," he told us that Ripon was the heartland of America. That first day, he escorted my mother and me along a field of pig corn. "Isn't it breathtaking?" he said. Ripon in the summer was gaudy with deceptiveness. The corn tassels sparkled, and June bugs shone on the stalks like emeralds. Frogs opened like purses on the stream banks, their gold eggs spilling into the water.

Nine months later, in spring, I bent my head against the ferocious wind and waded through the snow burying the graveyard that lies between Union Street and the college. There in the cemetery, I saw my father with the student with whom he would eventually run off. They stood against a gravestone set apart from the others that read HONEST JOHN WILLIAMS—A NEGRO. The girl was tall and willowy, and had hair like corn silk. My father pushed her against the gravestone and kissed her chin. She threw back her head and laughed—a little girl laugh, more childish than any sound I remembered ever having made around him.

"You make me feel like a king," he told her.

She wrapped her arm around his waist, as they walked down the hill away from the college. I shadowed them. My father was wearing a light green hat I had given him for Christmas, and ahead of me he looked wavering, insubstantial, ghoulish. I followed them along the back road that runs toward Union Street, and listened to the rise and fall of their voices. They disappeared into a field. I stood for a long time on the edge, waiting for them to return, but I had lost them in the darkness.

I never told my mother. She was busy striving to further my father's career. She went to every college function and cooked dinner for leering, wolfish professors and their thin-lipped wives. She attended the Lutheran church the dean belonged to, even though she was raised Catholic. She typed my father's papers and found a part-time job in Oshkosh at a knitwear outlet so that he could dedicate summers to his studies.

My mother first learned from a letter with a Montreal postmark what Mrs. Wallington had long known. The letter said, simply:

> April 15, 1973
>
> My darling wife—
>
> Because of circumstances over which I have no power, I have decided to relinquish my career and leave Ripon, and will not be returning. I know you have realized for some time how unbearable things are between us. There are two terrible mistakes in life. The first is to fall passionately in love with someone whom you learn, eventually, that you do not like. The second is to stay with someone whom you like and respect, but whom you cannot love. Keep this in mind in the months ahead—I want you to make good choices and to someday feel the joyousness that I do now. In my own experience, I believe that the second mistake is worse—but both are truly hellish. I hold you fondly in my thoughts.

My mother read and reread this letter: I know that the sentences scrambled and unscrambled themselves nonsensically before her eyes. That she asked herself, which was she: a woman he loved but did not like, or liked but did not love?

There did not seem to be any men in Ripon through whom my mother could discover the anguish of either hell. She did not think that college boys fifteen years her junior were a proper or realistic source of romance. I came to believe that girls should band together in some kind of international boycott, refusing to sleep with men more than a day older than us, forcing them all to turn to women their own age, or older. There was no other way to fight the terrible inequity in how some men could hog the whole of life and leave the rest of us with an empty dish.

My mother became desperate. Her friends would hardly look at her. She, a woman left to raise a child alone, was their worst fear. They were more afraid of her than their own deaths. She began working full-time in the knit-wear plant, and attending night school to get a teacher's certificate. For a while, my father telephoned us monthly, but then even his calls ended. The silence in our house became deafening: Before my sixteenth birthday, it drove my mother from home on many evenings, and on some nights, she did not return at all.

And how did this affect me, the daughter left behind? After a while, on those nights I did not come home either. Love grabbed hold of me in a terrible way in that period. I fought against it, but when it held me fast and laughed, I saw how weak I had become through the simple act of turning from a girl into a woman. My whole life, I had been thin and wiry and tough. I could fight any boy as an equal, leaping on him to wrestle and anchoring his elbows with my knees, or if he did the same to me, tossing him off with a smart hip twist. Late in high school, my body changed on me. No longer streamlined and otterlike in water, it swelled outward: hipward, assward, breastward. When I ran through the woods, it struggled behind me. When I passed through doors, my hips caught on the jambs, widening me.

On the nights my mother went out, I'd go to South

Woods or the shack in Kiwanis Park, smoking reefer and being felt up by boys from Green Lake or Omro or Oshkosh, or feeling them up. I finally made love with one who had a condom: his name was Rudolph Calemeyer, if it interests you, and he was passing through on his way to Racine. It was a winter night, and we were out on the ice at Green Lake with our flashlights. We looked down into a well dug by an ice fisherman: a green armless sleeve reaching toward oblivion. The sight of it and the icy quiet around us made us cling to each other. We unzipped our coats and zipped them to each other, then lay down in the chill wind. We worked fast. Our outer parts froze and we couldn't feel anything but him inside of me.

I heard about this event a month later when I started working in the Piggly Wiggly, although no one could have seen us, so far out on the ice in the pitch blackness. Sometimes, in the Piggly Wiggly, I heard about my mother as well: I learned all the insulting and envious names that had ever been invented for women.

By age nineteen, I had risen in the ranks at the Piggly Wiggly, and operated one of the cash registers. This is one of the reasons my life was destined to become interwoven with Milton Shekailo's. My job required me to wear a pink dress and white nurse's shoes, and I was looking for a way to escape it. Only my efforts to get fired and my job's continuing precariousness let me believe that the road ahead would take me far from the Piggly Wiggly and Ripon.

By the time I met Milton, I was ringing up cans in mint condition as half-priced dented purchases. I could be depended on not to see anyone pilfering gum and candy near the checkout line, so that all June children hovered around my register like yellow jackets. I weighed obese purple cabbages and hefty rutabagas, tipping up the scale so that they registered as frail as parsley. For a whole afternoon, I wore my pink uniform backwards, the Peter Pan collar looking priestly. I thought I was hysterical. That day, I was sent home with a warning that I'd be fired if there was any more trouble: from a glassed-in booth behind me, the supermarket manager, Mr. Boikus, watched the cashiers and commented over a microphone on our appearance or packaging speed, or to tell us he wasn't paying us to talk.

I knew from a conversation I had heard over by the sauerkraut that Mr. Boikus, the son of a retired minister, had at one time left Ripon to become a racetrack hanger-on, and professional gambler. In his youth, cometlike, he had made brief periodic visits to the town, dressed in fine clothes and, once, a diamond stickpin. Then his mother died when a cattle truck spun over the ice, capsizing and spilling steers onto the passenger side of the Ford which contained her. Mr. Boikus returned to Ripon to care for his father, and gave up gambling.

That was when the flame went out of Mr. Boikus. He became increasingly morose, this behavior hitting rock bottom when he found a temporary management position at the Piggly Wiggly, to last until the regular manager recovered from an operation. When Mr. Boikus spoke to me, it was only to say, "Young lady, you're late once again," or "You can walk straight home, Miss Henry, and give some thought to pride in your job." Stilted, empty phrases, worse even than silence. It was hard for me to picture Mr. Boikus in the days of his youth, vivacious and glittering as he bent over his pink racing forms.

The afternoon Milton Shekailo entered the supermarket, I was on my fourth day of wearing shitkickers, wide-soled and comfortable work boots molded by black mud and shoe leather oil to the shape of my foot, and twined with seasoned rawhide laces. If Mr. Boikus noticed my shoes, I planned to tell him that they increased my efficiency and brightened my personality, that shoes have a direct bearing on the human mind, more than your family history or genes: put on pointy high heels, and you feel like a silly, defenseless thing; in sneakers, you're free and careless; a strong pair of boots makes you indomitable; the nurse's shoes the Piggly Wiggly demanded made you fearful that the future offered you no promises, that life would be full of idiot bosses and adventurelessness.

Mr. Boikus noticed my shitkickers for the first time when Milton Shekailo's entrance into the supermarket pulled me like a riptide from behind the cashier's counter to get a better look at a handwritten notice he was tacking to the bulletin board. "Experienced Painter Wanted—Contact Milton or Daisy Shekailo," it said, followed by an address and telephone number. Mrs. Wallington and Mrs. Bozeman entered behind Milton Shekailo, and read the notice over my shoulder.

"Miss Henry," Mr. Boikus called from his glassed-in booth, a tone of doom in his voice. "I wish to see you briefly after work today. But briefly." Mrs. Wallington examined my white hose where they descended into my shitkickers. I sensed the rumblings of change, the future opening. I reread the notice and decided then that I would quit before I could be fired.

Milton Shekailo took a cart and wandered into the aisles, and Mrs. Wallington and Mrs. Bozeman followed at a careful distance. I returned to my register, but I watched him appear and disappear behind the pickle jars, peering at the liverwurst. I found myself hoping, inexplicably, that Milton Shekailo would choose my register. Perhaps he attracted me because I had never seen him before. Although his deep-set eyes and prominent browbone marked him as local stock, the fact that I had never met him made Milton Shekailo seem like a door to the unknown, a passport out of Wisconsin.

There were few faces in Ripon that I could not put a name to. And although the town would deny it, I knew something about everyone there. I had spent many weeks watching Daisy Shekailo shopping at the Piggly Wiggly. She had dark eyes ringed by shadows. She was short and sinewy, with black hair: she struck me as looking the way I assumed I would when I got older.

I also knew that her husband, Milton, worked long and erratic hours in Fond du Lac as a maintenance man, and was rarely seen in town. He had bought a barn last owned by Mr. Shutz, a gentleman farmer famous for prize-winning hogs he treated better than Ripon treated most of its people. Rumor had it, for example, that he had kept his pigs on immaculate cement, and hosed them down daily. I had seen the hogs, white with slender ankles and long eyelashes, lounging around their water hole. They reminded me of Turkish harem girls I had examined in an art book the school library later removed from the shelves.

Nevertheless, the man who drove the chicken truck to the Piggly Wiggly had told me one day, while unloading the white and fluttering chickens in their wire cages, that Shutz had grown tired of his hogs, slaughtered them, and moved to Chicago. He had trouble selling his land afterwards because the barn could not be insured against fire. I could see it from my mother's house—a huge wooden structure with towering German arches. The insurance companies favored the modern, aluminum-sided barns. After two years, at the beginning of spring, Milton Shekailo had moved in and stocked the barn with regular pigs, the kind bought and sold as pork chops at the Piggly Wiggly.

I was ruminating over this information when Milton reappeared from the back of the store, his cart heaped too high with groceries. He stopped twice to pick up a box of butter that slid from a towering pile of canned goods in the cart's front compartment. He saw me watching him and waved, before Mrs. Wallington and Mrs. Bozeman cut him off from view and he disappeared into the bread section.

Mrs. Bozeman went right for my register, and Mrs. Wallington followed, talking a blue streak. Mrs. Bozeman unloaded her cart lethargically, and kept her eyes fixed on the prices as I rang up each item. She never turned to Mrs. Wallington, or acknowledged that she was listening. But I saw how she soaked up every word like a new mop.

"Wouldn't you know it, I went up there in the Book Mobile to welcome Mrs. Shekailo to town," Mrs. Wallington began. That's her job, driving this Winnebago filled with books around Ripon. The Book Mobile is a sort of self-styled welcome wagon, her excuse to knock on people's doors and worm into their lives. "I virtually died when I walked by the barn. The smell! Mr. Shutz never kept his pigs that way. He cleaned their pens regularly. So I rang the bell, and Mrs. Shekailo doesn't get up to answer, just calls out from wherever she's sitting to come in.

Which I do. There she is sprawled on the couch, drinking a six-pack. The children running around like wild animals, and her just ignoring them, sipping from a beer can without bothering to undo it from the empty can its joined to with one of those plastic rings.

" 'Can I help *you*?' she says.

"I would have sat down, but the armchair was piled up with junk. An empty feed sack. Her purse, all spilled out on the chair. A jar of peanut butter. But it was the smell, let me tell you, that almost knocked me off my feet. A pig smell. I've never smelled such a smell in my life. It wasn't coming from the barn either—it was all over the room.

" 'Mrs. Shekailo,' I said, 'won't you come to my house for lunch tomorrow?'

" 'No place to put the boys,' she said. 'But maybe another time. I'd like that. I need a place to put the boys first.'

"I never saw her again though. After I left, I swear I could smell that pig manure on me all day, as if I'd rolled in it. Later on, Melissa told me that once she sat behind Mrs. Shekailo at the school play, and do you know what? Melissa had to slide over a seat because the odor was so strong. And afterward, she said she could still actually smell it on her own dress. 'Imagine, if you had her over, she'd leave your kitchen stinking like a pig,' she told me."

"I'll put those back," Mrs. Bozeman said, suspiciously, after I'd charged her for some TV dinners.

"That's not all. One night I was at Moxie's with Melissa, and this army officer from Green Bay told us that pig smell has a special property that makes it cling to things. Your hair. Your cotton shirt. He said the army did experiments with it. They mixed it with pheromones. They threw this smell into foxholes onto soldiers, so that when they crawled out of the ditches these special moths would track them, because of their smell, or something like that. Because the smell would stick to them like glue, and these special moths were attracted to it."

She shut up when Milton Shekailo parked his cart behind her. Now let me tell you what Mrs. Wallington had in her shopping cart: feminine hygiene spray; twelve one-quart bottles of Coca-Cola; Tater Tots; corn on the cob; two dozen boxes butterscotch pudding; a sack of Rippin' Good Cookies—the ones shaped like windmills; a romance novel and *Twelve Diets That Work;* and four cans Vienna sausage (one for forty cents, three for a dollar).

When Milton Shekailo parked behind her, Mrs. Wallington pretended to browse through a *Good Housekeeping* on the rack above the counter, but all along, she was sneaking looks at him. After she picked up her grocery bags, she walked out of the store sideways, craning her neck around to see him.

Milton Shekailo unloaded his groceries not one at a time, but in armfuls. He had a sulfurous smell, manure combined with his own pungent manliness, and when he plunked two coils of binding cord on the belt, his hands looked huge, like two roasts. I had an impulse to weigh them on my scale and ring them up on my register.

As soon as Milton Shekailo had paid me, Mr. Boikus called through his microphone, "Miss Henry. Change your shoes this instant and come up here." I made a helpless gesture, shrugging my shoulders and pointing to show that I was unwilling to abandon a customer.

"Hire me," I said to Milton as I counted out his change.

"I know how to paint, I'm dependable, and I have the shoes." I held up one of my shitkickers.

Milton grinned at me. He looked in his late thirties, and was broad and hulking and hairy: black curls poked from the front and back of his V-neck undershirt. His face was dark with whiskers struggling to escape. He was the kind of man whose beard would cling to him like a luxurious, minky animal. I myself would have been hairy if I had been a man. I have a soft brush of black down rimming my top lip, which I've never bleached. It has an alluring paradoxical quality, a mustache, but softly feminine.

"OK. Eight o'clock tomorrow," he told me. "I'll probably be in the back of the barn." He circled four grocery bags with his arms and picked them up as if they were one. He walked backwards out of the store, nodding at the manager.

That was my last day at the Piggly Wiggly. For the first time since my father had left, I was thrown back on my own devices to find out what I needed to know. Perhaps that is why I walked so blindly through the next part of my life.

He wasn't there. Daisy Shekailo answered the door, and two black-haired boys, no more than four and five years old, peered around her hips through the screen door. They wore electric orange caps and under the visors their eyes were deep-set and cast into shadow. They had shoulders too broad for their ages, bulky arms and legs, square hands.

The smaller one leaned toward me and said, "Who?"

"I don't know where Milton is," Daisy told me.

She stood there, and I stood there, and then she stood there some more.

"Did he leave paint for me?" I asked.

"No. There's some paint scrapers by the barn. Stay *there,* Daniel," she told the older boy, who was inching past her out the door. "I really don't know what he means to do with the barn, it's stupid to paint it."

This made me feel pretty nervous about my work. "Maybe you could just show me where the scrapers are," I suggested.

"Cut it the hell out," she told Daniel. He was doing something that made the screen door behind her jiggle, something that made a scraping noise. He stopped. "Sit over on the sofa with Jake and don't turn the TV up high. I want to see you there when I get back." She stepped outside and the screen door closed loud as a gunshot behind her.

I followed her to the barn. With each step, I realized that Mrs. Wallington's words had not begun to approximate the potency of those pigs' sulfurous and hellish stench. From twenty-five feet away, its ammonias burned my throat and made my eyes tear. Even this did not prepare me for the shock of what I saw when we entered the barn. Where there had once been the immaculate gleaming Shutz hogs, monstrous animals now churned and milled in the barn's darkness. The Shekailo pigs were filthy and elephantine. They moved everywhere, ankle deep in black sludge, in jerry-rigged pens built from scrap wood and old machine parts twined together with barbed wire.

A sow, hulking and hairless, with long, heavy nipples, heaved herself to her feet and stuck her nose between two slats of wood. She threw off a pure smell of rotten eggs, but up close, she had the same long-lashed society woman eyes as Shutz's pigs. She peered at us with curiosity, and ran her nose back and forth between the wood slats, pinching it where the slats intersected in a snarl of wire. Daisy lifted a long pole with a U-shaped piece of iron attached to the end, hooked the pole around the sow's nose, and pushed it toward a wide opening between the slats. The sow slid her nose from the fence and whirled backward into the darkness.

"The pigs are so stupid they get their snouts caught in the fence," Daisy explained. "So we have this snout pole to shove them back out." She laid the snout pole against the wall: the iron at the top was rusty and twisted, like ancient weaponry.

"Daisy!" one of the boys called from the house. "Daisy, hey Daisy! Jake's messing with me."

"Christ," she said to no one at all. Then she pointed at a plastic bucket. "Look in there. I got to watch Milton's kids."

I found two new scrapers, still in their wrappers. "The boys aren't yours?" I asked her.

"No," she said. "No, they sure as hell aren't. Milton's ex-wife lives down the road. I babysit the kids on weekdays and most weekends. They're a handful." She turned back toward the house. "Maybe Milton's at the paint store," she relented, before leaving me alone.

The barn's arches rose forty feet overhead—the task before me seemed a feat I was not expected to accomplish, whose purpose was to alter me by showing me the limits of my character. I extended the ladder as far as it would go, anchored its legs with cinder blocks, and scaled to the top. I looked through a small opening cut high in the wall.

Below, frenetic shapes roiled and gleamed in the shadows of the barn. The pigs looked treacherous, a school of carnivorous sea animals waiting for me to pitch downward into their element.

I worked all day, scraping off flakes of red paint, the pigs' penetrating odors wafting from below. Milton Shekailo never showed up. Daisy did not come out to offer me lunch at noon, and I grew dizzy, mesmerized by the pig smell and my own methodical motions high above the pigsties. Once, Jake and Daniel entered the barn, their electric orange caps flickering below me. Daniel leaned forward and emptied a box into one of the pens. His hat fell off as a flurry of crackers descended over a group of pigs. The animals lunged toward the boys, and from where I sat on the ladder, the boys looked in mortal danger, with nothing but the necklace of jerry-rigged fence between them and the animals.

"Looky them," said Daniel, standing on the fence. Jake crawled up beside his brother, and the two stood together, watching the pigs eat. Daniel picked up the snout pole and tried to maneuver his hat toward the fence, but a large sow got in the way.

"Forget it," Jake told him. "It'll stink up your head." He took the pole and scratched the sow's back.

"Hi, Nora," he said.

"The pig's name is Nora?" I called down at them.

Jake looked up and waved. "Daniel lost his hat," he called back.

Afterward, the two brothers lingered at the barn door, as if they had been told to return immediately to the house. Jake pushed over a bucket of water, and Daniel threw a rock at a bottle in the doorway, barely missing it. Then they cut back to the house and ran inside.

An hour later, the boys emerged, wearing triangular hats folded from grocery bags. Daisy opened the door, and handed Daniel a child's lunch box, murmuring something I could not hear. He ran to my ladder, holding his brown paper hat in place with his free hand. "Daisy made us helmets!" he said, leaning the lunch box against the ladder. He raced to the house before I could thank him. The box contained three peanut butter and jelly sandwiches, a banana, a box of gingersnaps, carrot sticks, a half pint of milk, and a note saying, "Sorry lunch is late. I hope it's not too hot up there. Take a break whenever you want to."

At 5:00, Daisy loaded the two boys, still wearing their brown paper hats, into an old white De Soto station wagon, and drove off down the highway. By 7:00, Daisy had not come back, and I walked home, cursing myself for having worked a full day without getting a day's wages. I decided I would return the next morning, demand my pay, and start looking for a new job.

It was not until I stepped inside the closed space of my mother's living room that I noted the smell: at first it seemed subtle, like a faint odor of gunpowder. Then suddenly it intensified to that sulfurous and hellish odor in the barn. It stuck to my hair, dusted the skin on my arms, clung to my shirt and socks. I undressed in the basement and tossed my clothes into the washing machine, showered, washing my hair twice, and soaked in the bathtub in my mother's Jean Naté oil. Still, after I had pulled on clean clothes, and started toward town, I smelled those pigs on me. The odor at times seemed to vanish, but then it would leap up suddenly, overpowering me.

At The Spot, the only bar in town, I ran into Joe Gurzeski, who'd dropped out of my high school class two years before. He told me he had some Boone's Farm strawberry wine in his truck, and we drove with it to his house. His parents were away at a square dancing tournament, and we ended up taking off all our clothes in their bedroom. Joe climbed on top of me, but before we had remembered how to fit ourselves together, he gasped and I felt a warm splash on my stomach. He poked his nose in my ear and told me, "You poor girl, you poor, poor girl." This made us both laugh so hard and loud we almost missed hearing his parents come into the house. If his father hadn't called out to locate him, I never would have vaulted through the bedroom window into the side yard in time to escape.

Kept to myself, this moment with Joe took on an unbearable sweetness by midmorning, as I walked down the highway toward the Shekailos'. I savored the moment as long as I could, because I knew that shortly, it would be picked up by a tornado of town gossip and turned into something mean and destructive.

When I entered the Shekailos' drive, I heard an argument coming from the barn. It was a one-way argument, with mostly Daisy talking.

"I won't stand it!" she shouted. I halted in the drive, and leaned against the De Soto. "You drag me to this goddamn Ripoff, Wisconsin, where I'm miles from the nearest house and can't find work, then make me babysit your kids all day while your goddamn wife studies art in that half-assed college—"

"Ex-wife. You're my wife, Day," Milton whispered. His whisper was loud, a muffled bellow.

"I'm human too! I have needs! Maybe I'd like to sit in

a classroom at the college and paint naked men all day too."

"I have to work! You know I have to work. Christ, what do you want me to do? What am I supposed to do?"

"Make your goddamn wife take care of her own kids."

"She's looking after them right now."

"For once. And who's taking care of me, I want to know? All you care about is those goddamn stinking pigs."

"They're money. These pigs are money."

"I want to go back to Milwaukee. You shouldn't have dropped out of school. You never told me it would be like this."

"I can't leave my kids again."

"You never see them. And you leave *me* alone all day!" Daisy ran from the barn to the De Soto. She yanked open the door and got in the driver's seat before she saw me leaning on the car.

"Move!" she told me, and I did.

Milton watched her drive off. Only then did he notice me. He turned and vanished into the barn.

I walked toward him, but stayed outside, on the fringes of the pig smell. "I worked here all yesterday," I called inside. "I didn't get paid."

Two suckling pigs snuffled along the fence. Milton emerged from the darkness, holding up two paint scrapers. His chest was enormous, shaped like a bull's head. "I'll pay you once a week, OK? I couldn't make it yesterday. I had to work an extra shift."

"OK," I said. The sullenness in my voice surprised me. I took a scraper and climbed up the ladder, thinking about Daisy. I peered through a knothole and, below me in the shadows, Daniel's orange hat glowed like an ember.

Milton leaned another ladder beside mine. As he climbed onto it, the rungs bowed under his massive feet. He scraped with exuberance, the paint peeling from his hand in flamboyant curls.

The next thing he told me was: "Winston Churchill praised pigs above other domestic animals, saying, 'Dogs look up to us. Cats look down on us. Pigs treat us as equals.' Pigs will eat anything, including pork chops. Once when I was eight, I personally witnessed a pig in Williamsburg, Virginia, eat a pair of sunglasses that fell off the father of my friend Brian Breneman, metal frames and all—"

I had to laugh. "All right," I said. "I love painting pig barns."

Milton spent the day enriching my knowledge of pigs. Pigs are the only animals which will drink until drunk, he explained. A pig cannot sweat, and will explode in the heat if he doesn't have mud to wallow in. Bacon grease, mixed with pine tar, is a superior dressing for keeping horse hooves from cracking. Scientists had designed a eugenic Nazi low-cholesterol lean meat pig clone that sold for a half million dollars as a stud, and then the farmer who bought him discovered that his piglets came out fat and ordinary, clinging to the laws of nature. A pig is the only mammal other than man that does not manufacture vitamin C. The valves of a pig's heart are the best replacements for human heart valves.

Around noon, the telephone rang, and Milton jumped to the ground. Under my ladder, the ground shook.

"I'll be right back," he called, heading for the house. I surveyed the barn: we had scraped a ridiculously small part of it.

Half an hour later, Milton returned, carrying a cooler and dressed in a dark green uniform with "Shekailo" stitched in orange over the pocket. "That was my boss. I have to go to work early. Here's lunch." He lifted the cooler's lid: it contained half a roast chicken, a sack of apples, a six-pack of Blatz beer, and three pieces of chocolate cake.

In early evening, the De Soto sped into the driveway, crunching the gravel. The boys burst from the car and disappeared. Daisy entered the house, came out almost immediately afterwards, and stood under my ladder.

"He went to work already?" she called up.

"His boss phoned."

"Shit," she said. She took a beer from the cooler, opened it, and leaned against the barn.

"Jake scraped his hand!" Daniel yelled. He and Jake emerged from behind the De Soto, Jake holding his arm.

"Let's see, mister," Daisy told him. "Let's wash that off." She took him into the barn and water rushed from the hose inside. "You'll be fine," Daisy said, leading him back to the cooler. "All you need is a medal for bravery." She sat on the cooler, and picked up a Blatz bottle cap from the ground. "You can wear a silver star." Jake and Daniel bent close to her as she pulled the cork center from the bottle cap, and held the cap against Jake's T-shirt. Then she slipped the cork inside his shirt and pressed it against the back of the cap, wedging the shirt in between so that the dull metal clung just beneath Jake's collar.

"There: a silver star," she told him.

"Man oh man," said Daniel.

"You two get in the house and wash up. Your dad's

not here. I just have to water the pigs, and then I'll take you to the A & W for hamburgers."

The boys shrieked and raced to the house. Daisy looked up at me and said, "Do you know what he clears on these pigs? One thousand lousy dollars a year, that's all. His salary all goes to his ex-wife, and she hardly spends a cent on the boys. We need every dime we can get." She paused, and then said, "I'm leaving him. Today. Tonight. I'm at the end of my rope."

I climbed down. From the ground, I saw how tired she looked: the rings under her eyes were dark blue, her clothes were wrinkled and her hair was even dirtier than mine.

"I'm only telling you this," Daisy said, "because there's no one else here to tell it to." She stepped inside the barn and I heard water filling a bucket.

I considered what she had said, and decided that I was the last person on the earth she needed to pour her heart out to. I could not see myself following a man to Ripon, Wisconsin, or anywhere else. I suspected I would lose my mind babysitting all day, and could not imagine living in an isolated farmhouse on the edge of a mean-minded town, caring for evil-smelling pigs.

I followed her into the barn. "I'm sorry" was all I said. "Where will you go?"

"My folks live in Oshkosh. Christ. I hate Oshkosh. You know where I want to live? Los Angeles—ha!"

Suddenly she felt terrifyingly familiar to me: in that instant, I feared that I could wake up one morning and discover that her life fit me as snugly as a Piggly Wiggly uniform. And in the same moment, it occurred to me that there were things which could not happen to me once I'd grown completely into a woman. I doubted I would ever find myself in Milton's shoes, for instance, marrying someone who would care for my children while I worked, just as I would never run off with a student half my age. This idea rankled inside of me. It was not a clear thought, and I was not sure of its significance. But when I next looked at Daisy filling a new bucket with the hose, I thought she looked mean and ugly, meaner and uglier than I ever would.

I saw that she was waiting for me to give her something, a word of sympathy or understanding, but I stayed silent.

Daisy turned off the spigot and coiled the hose. Inside the darkness of the barn, the pigs glimmered and flashed like phantoms. The sow the boys called Nora stepped toward us out of the darkness, watching us with those society woman eyes. Her nose pushed between the slats, snuffling into a half knothole far up one slat, exploring the air outside the pen. And then her nose stuck. The hog pulled backwards, and her nose lengthened, but remained caught in the knothole. She gazed up at us, looking surprised and embarrassed.

"Jesus, not again," Daisy said. She picked up the snout pole and placed it alongside the sow's nose. As she did, the hog turned into a different animal, squealing and charging the fence. I saw then that instead of trying to push the hog's snout free, Daisy was pinching it against the wires where the wood slats intersected. She leaned on the pole.

The hog jumped as if electrified, and screamed in that way pigs have—a sound of protest so pure and unmistakable, I wondered what human could approximate it.

"You're pushing the wrong way!" I shouted, but the

sow's voice was deafening. Daisy wore an expression of absolute concentration: she was locked in mortal combat with the animal. Tears spilled from her eyes as she clenched the pole in both hands, throwing her weight behind it.

"God damn you!" she shouted. "God damn you to hell!"

"Daisy, stop it! Stop it!" I yelled, grabbing the pole. We fell backwards as the hog—a great shape swirling in the dark sea of the barn—freed herself. Daisy toppled onto me, and for a moment, her face was so close to mine that I could smell her—a fragrant, womanly smell. A hot tear fell from her face onto my neck. Then she pushed away and ran from the barn.

From an invisible corner, the sow's shadowy shape emerged and stood motionless. She looked at me warily, snorted, startled some straw upward with her nose, then turned and flashed backward into the barn's chaos.

After that, weeks passed before I saw Daisy again. Milton fed and watered the pigs twice daily, and worked in the barn Saturdays and most weekday mornings, when he did not have to do a double shift at his maintenance job. Each day, he looked more exhausted, and the first week, he must have slept in his clothes because they were wrinkled beyond imagination. Then he stopped shaving and his black beard swelled over his face until I could no longer remember what he looked like.

He told me that the boys were being cared for by his mother in Fond du Lac, and that Daisy was staying in Oshkosh. After that, he said little. For days, he scraped the towering walls with relentless silence. I tried prodding him into speech, but I could not draw out the man who had talked so extravagantly about pigs. He resisted every question.

"What did you study in school?"

"I never finished."

"What did you study?"

"The usual."

"What?"

"Animal husbandry and Spanish."

"How do you say 'pig' in Spanish?"

"*Puerco,* and other words."

"What other words?"

"*Cochino. Cerdo. Marrano.*"

"Is Daisy coming back?"

"She hates my kids."

"She doesn't."

"It's over."

"How can you tell?"

No answer.

Milton started working on the ground far below me, where he did not have to make conversation. He scraped meticulously, sanding minor irregularities for whole minutes, running his fingers along the wood to test its smoothness. We entered a rhythm of work, monotonous and emptying. My whole being became a vision of rough wood, a rasping sound, the lull of my hardening muscles pushing the scraper over the barn's endless surface, the redolent pigs below.

At first, the thought of Daisy worried me like a splinter. I wondered what she was doing, whether she was working, how she was getting by without Milton. But gradually, I pulled the image of her from my mind, and then I forgot her entirely.

I started thinking instead about Milton. Each evening, he paid me a day's wages, saying nothing more than "Here" when he did so. The pig smell was in the bills he handed me, and it clung to me all the time now. It was on my socks, when I pulled them from the depths of my drawers. It was inside my pillowcases, on the armchair from which I watched television. At night when I closed my eyes, I felt as if I were swaying from the great height of the ladder, while below me the white pigs glimmered, their humpbacks rising and falling in the darkness. And then Milton would appear: his plow yoke shoulders and his massive hands, the dense beard behind which he hid his gigantic and mysterious silences.

Spending all day with a person who wouldn't speak unnerved me. Restlessness filled my hands like water scurrying from a tap. After work, I drove for hours over the back roads. Soon August would be darkening the edges of things, making the mornings rise late and condensed over the fields. My savings were piling up, and I thought of my grandmother and my cousin, Stanley, in Jersey City. There, summer would still be expanding fatly on the hot cement steps of her apartment building.

One day when I stopped in Oshkosh for gasoline, Daisy Shekailo pulled up beside me. She waved and opened her car window. She had lost weight and was wearing too much makeup.

"How's Milton?" she asked.

"Sad and quiet. I think he misses you a lot."

"I hardly feel alive without him." She paused and then asked, "Who's watching the boys?"

"His mother, mostly. I haven't seen them for a while."

Daisy looked thoughtful, rolled up the window, and drove off.

* * *

At the end of twenty-seven days, the barn was gray, stripped clean, and ready for painting. Milton arrived on a Sunday with a truckload of paint he had purchased at a discount from his job. The sight of the cans and brushes startled me. Surely, I thought, there must be another way to paint a barn—we could borrow a giant spray gun like the airbrush I had seen an art professor from the college using in his backyard. Milton pried the lid off the first can: the paint was clay red. We spread the dirtying color back over the barn. The turpentine entered my head, the paint smell mingling with the odor of the pigs. We worked quietly until nightfall.

He drove me home. When his truck stopped in front of the house, he opened his door, and looked at me in the light thrown from the cab ceiling. Paint was in my hair, on my T-shirt and pants and shitkickers.

"You look like a grub," he said.

"Thanks," I answered, climbing down from the truck.

"A pretty grub," he bellowed after me.

I swear to you, I did not want to mess around with Milton Shekailo. That night, I thought about Daisy, how much she must be missing Milton, how it was too early to get between them. I believed if I betrayed her, I would be betraying myself. But in those days, I couldn't see when love was sneaking up on me. How does love grab other people? With me, it's physical as instinct—my temperature rises and stays there, the skin on my arms burns and my blood runs through my arteries like a fast car. The next day, these things started happening whenever I looked at Milton painting below me, his huge chest descending into his shirt. Still, I kept my feelings to myself.

I didn't know that town rumors had already circulated. That they had been collecting for weeks, starting in the Piggly Wiggly and traveling outward from there as mere suspicions and theories, mean titters, and nods of disapproval, settling temporarily in Mrs. Bozeman's variety store, and then moving on. By the time I heard them, the rumors had become elaborate and believable, and what they basically amounted to was that I had broken up Daisy and Milton's marriage.

The story first grabbed me from behind when I was loitering by the shoelaces in the variety store. I heard Mrs. Wallington's voice behind the embroidery counter. I caught only a few words. "Home wrecker," and then "her mother's example," and I knew immediately that this had something to do with me. I set down a package of rawhide laces, and heard: "popping that girl in the barn every night. His wife's at her wit's end. Mr. Boikus had to fire her for carrying on with the man who delivered the chickens." I backed out of the store.

Daisy heard the rumors too, but in a less developed form, or perhaps she could not read the clues as well as I could, since when she visited me, she didn't know the name of the girl Milton was said to be playing around with. Daisy appeared at my mother's house after work three days later, thinking I might know who Milton was seeing. And that's when, without knowing it, Daisy told me that she was going to kill me.

The next morning, I informed Milton I wanted two days off. I drove down to Milwaukee, spent the night in the Y, visited the zoo and wandered around small museums, browsed in bookstores and bought *Wisconsin Death Trip*, popular at the time. I watched two showings back to back of *Midnight Cowboy,* my first X-rated film. Nothing that I saw that weekend seemed as complex or disastrous as my own life rushing to greet me. I promised myself I would quit my painting job and look for temporary work during canning season at the Jolly Green Giant.

I didn't do either of those things. I returned to the barn, and as soon as I laid eyes on Milton, I knew that what I had heard in the variety store was true. That I could sooner elude my own death than the inexorable certainty of Mrs. Wallington's knowledge.

How did it happen? He drove me home a second time. I told him my mother was away for the summer, and invited him in for a beer, thinking: he hardly knows me at all. We pulled off our boots at the door. He sat on my mother's sofa, gingerly, as if afraid he could break it, and spoke very little. He looked heavy with loss. In the corner of the living room, a cricket shrilled like a police whistle. I placed my hand on top of his massive hand.

"Don't, Netta," he said. "You have no idea what kind of man I am. I mess up everything I touch. It's no good." Despite this warning, what we both did next was to stand up and take off our pants.

I can't tell you what was going through my head at that moment: perhaps nothing. An ex-colleague of my father's, a retired professor of behavioral psychology, heard the rumors, and rumors of his theories returned to their source. He thought that a young girl abandoned by her father will seek out father figures for vengeance, and wreak havoc on intact homes whenever possible.

I don't put much stock in such an easy explanation. If he bothered to ask me, I'd tell him what this story is really about is how a person's internal order can be broken down without warning, as if your whole self were just an imposter of who you are. It is about how before this experience, I had been composed of a certain toughness, a toughness with a completeness and coherence to it. And how afterwards, I lost that coherence, and replaced it with something at once larger and less whole. Later, my mother would say, "Oh *Hon*ey," holding me to her and persuading me to get on a Greyhound to Jersey City because, she said, she did not "want to live to see me broken in two." Or, she added, "cut to pieces by Daisy Shekailo," whom my mother pictured as a sort of raving madwoman after what she would end up doing, although Milton would forgive Daisy enough to ask her to come back months later, when she would refuse him.

Perhaps the most accurate view, however, was that of Mrs. Wallington, whose malevolent wisdom drew from the multifaceted vicissitudes of her vicarious life. She thought that Milton and I showed an utter lack of judgment, a chaos of morals, in which neither I nor Milton had any idea what we were doing, and which no amount of philosophizing might explain in retrospect.

Mrs. Wallington added that Milton and I would both be lucky if we weren't shot dead, and that she did not know what was worse, someone who purposely kills himself, as she strongly believed Buster Dodge had when he froze to death sleeping in Kiwanis Park; or someone who treats his life with profound negligence, say a man like Lars Johnsen who pulls dead drunk onto an icy highway; or someone who walks blindly into domestic bliss without any appreciation of its dangers. Mrs. Wallington reasoned that all were sad situations, but that none was more disturbing than that of a girl who gets involved with a married man, in the very house his wife should be living in, when his wife is known to walk Main Street asking questions and resenting him more each day, a wife whom the girl knows, not well perhaps, but at least by more than name and face.

As Milton kissed me, he unbuttoned my shirt, rubbing my nipples with his sandpapery thumbs. He moved his mouth down my body in large kisses, making smacking noises with his lips, so loud they defied embarrassment. He grazed like a large, slow animal. His huge tongue moved back and forth between my legs until he felt an explosion, and then, moaning, he pulled himself over me as I loosened and opened. He had a control and staying power that I had not found yet in myself or the boys I knew. He lumbered tirelessly over me, forward and backwards. I felt a large, frantic animal leap out of me and burst into nothingness. Sweat eddied around his whiskers and splashed on my stomach until he cried out. Our smell filled the room.

There and then, I knew it would have been better if I had hooked up with a local boy, who could have convinced me that love was nothing more than a fumbling, sweetly embarrassing thing. Because Milton scared me—I worried then that I might go the rest of my life without finding other men who made love like that, that the memory of him would pursue me from one man to the next, forcing me into comparisons that filled me with hunger and longing.

We carried on for the whole month of August, making it on the bare boards of a crawl space at the top of the barn, in his truck, in South Woods and the shack in Kiwanis Park. It is hard to say if we ever really got to know each other. Once, I asked him to describe himself, and he said that he no longer knew who he was. That he felt like a man between lives, with the next life nowhere in sight.

In the afternoons, when he left for his job in Fond du Lac, my body flared and leaned toward the highway, as if it wanted to separate itself from me. I hemmed it in and it took me over. I no longer thought of escape.

In late August, as I walked toward the Piggly Wiggly, I spotted a woman who reminded me of Daisy Shekailo, small and dark, emerging from the store with two gallon cans of barbecue lighter fluid. I wasn't certain if it was her: she was walking fast and hooded against the hardening wind.

After I entered the Piggly Wiggly, I felt someone shadowing me through the frozen food section. Mr. Boikus. He sidled up beside me and pretended to inspect some lima beans. His necktie rested like a black tongue on the frozen corn.

"Netta," he said. He had never called me by my first name. "Your mother told me you might be leaving Ripon and perhaps going to college."

How did Mr. Boikus know my mother?

"Don't disappoint her," he said, and then added, "Your mother deserves better. I know it's none of my business, but your mother is a fine lady and your father is a slime-necked bastard for doing her the way he did. Your mother is the most beautiful woman I've ever known."

I did not want to hear any more. "You're right," I said. "It's not your business."

"Netta," he called after me as I retreated toward the electric doors. "Watch yourself."

I walked to the college and bought some reefer from an

arriving student. I smoked until Mr. Boikus's voice disappeared from my mind, and then I headed home. When Milton came over, we smoked three more joints after we took our clothes off. But the reefer worked the wrong way, making my head feel cottony and disconnected from my body. I watched Milton from a great height, as he seemed to be kissing a hip that did not belong to me. I had no edge, no place to hold on to, and we both fell asleep somewhere in the middle. When I woke up a few hours later, Milton lay on his side, his back to me.

Out the window, the sky was pinkening and reddening over the hill where Milton's barn stood. I looked at the clock: it said 4:00 A.M., too early for an August sunrise. I showered and pulled on my pants, holding Milton's image carefully in my mind, like a cup of water filled so high that it might spill over any moment. I slipped on Milton's shirt, and its manurey smell embraced me as I stepped outside. The sky over his barn turned a brilliant orange.

I opened my mouth to call his name, but I could not remember it. I ran inside the house and shook him. "The barn's on fire! Shit, get up! The fire's so big you can see it from here!"

We ran up that hill—but by the time we arrived, the roof timbers and walls were collapsing in bright piles. The fire had raged for hours. No one had been bold enough to appear at my mother's house to fetch Milton. Onlookers told us that swallows had flared from the windows, and that the pigs had died noiselessly in their sleep. Milton and I watched until long after the fire trucks left and the last people came to view the fallen and glowing timbers.

By afternoon, the charred rectangles of stalls darkened the ground neatly, as if a blueprint of the fire's anger. Here and there lay the bodies of sows lulled to death by smoke, with rows of burnt black suckling pigs lined evenly as teeth beside them. As the last people gathered, Milton pulled me toward him, and folded his arms in front of me.

I saw Daisy emerge from the circle of onlookers. She fixed her eyes on me long enough to understand what kind of woman I was, what I was doing there with Milton. But she looked right through and beyond me, unrecognizing. Her rage was that enormous: it didn't have a target or focus, it was larger than me, larger than Milton, or the both of us.

STANLEY

THE GOLDEN CAR

IT WAS an ordinary Saturday—the kind that made Arthurine Ray long for something to happen—sunny and cheerful and dull, the children thundering in the background. She leaned out the kitchen window, and spied on her grandson, Stanley. He had arrived in New Orleans at the end of July, silent and watchful beside his mother as she had cried and pleaded, "Stanley's not safe with me, Mama. Ross won't think to come here. He wouldn't even guess you and I'd be on talking terms. I'll come get Stanley when the coast is clear and me and Buddy are all settled in Florida." That had been weeks ago.

Now Stanley braced himself for an attack, standing with his legs apart on a hill of dirt left by some road workers.

"I am king of this dirt pile!" his cousin, Netta, shouted

from below as she fended off Roy, a neighbor's boy Arthurine babysat on weekends.

"I am—" Stanley echoed.

"No, you're not!" Netta screamed as she and Roy butted Stanley in the back of the knees. Stanley seemed to snap like a twig and flew to the bottom of the pile.

Stanley, who had just turned five, was Roy's age and Netta's size but, Arthurine noted, no match for either of them. Roy was a hulking five-year-old built like a heavyweight boxer. Netta, at six, was small and wiry and unbreakable, and on the frequent occasions when her mother needed a rest and sent her to Arthurine's for a visit, Netta awed Stanley with her brassiness. Stanley had a dishonest kind of tallness that had left him stretched thin and flimsy. He rarely caused trouble, and while Arthurine could always tell what the children were up to by listening for Netta's high-pitched shouts, Stanley so rarely made noise that at times Arthurine felt she had no handle on who the person was at the center of him. How could anyone ever get to know him, when he talked so little? He was nothing like his mother, who unraveled the secret of who she was in a minute by chattering on and on.

He looked like his father, Ross Wilkes, an impossibly tall insurance salesman who had been rough with women and silent around men. Arthurine thought it was a sign of life's bad sense of humor that Stanley took after a father he had not seen in years. It was as if Wilkes could exert his evil influence from wherever he might be. Stanley had Wilkes's russet hair, and his face too—a narrow rectangle with the features crowded so close together that he appeared cross-eyed.

"I am the king of America!" Netta's shout cut Arthurine's thought in half. Stanley pulled Netta backward by the hair, but she dug her toes into the dirt and pushed him over. "I am the king of Alabama! I am the king of Egypt!" she gasped.

Roy and Stanley grabbed Netta from behind in two half nelsons and dragged her to the bottom of the dirt pile. Netta began crawling back up, but Roy fended her off from the middle of the pile and Stanley grabbed her by the ankle.

"You big ugly fat loud lousy bastards!" Netta yelled, kicking at Stanley.

Netta pushed Roy hard enough to send him past Stanley. "I am Jesus Christ!" Netta said from above, baring her arm and flexing her muscles.

Stanley shrieked with wicked joy.

"I am Jesus Christ!" echoed Roy, pounding his chest.

"I AM JESUS CHRIST!" Netta hollered at the top of her lungs.

"You shut that up!" Arthurine called.

The children turned in unison toward Arthurine—an angry old woman framed in the kitchen window. Her crow-colored hair lifted and resettled as a gust of wind blew over the sill.

Roy waved back at Arthurine with a friendly expression as if he were a senator riding in a convertible in the middle of a parade. Netta ignored her and threw an acorn across Prytania Street. Stanley copied Netta as she pretended to pull pins from more acorns and made the sound of grenades detonating. The acorns soared over the street and hit a blue car. The children circled the house to move beyond the view of the kitchen.

Arthurine's neighbor Mrs. Sophie Pulley (whom

Arthurine referred to as Wind Bag) peered around the corner of her house, separated from Arthurine's by a narrow side yard. Wind Bag's dog, an ugly liver-spotted dalmatian, howled from underneath Arthurine's newly waxed Cadillac, where the animal had been lying all day to avoid the heat. A golden car approached and parked alongside the Prytania Theater across the street. It was a fancy car, a Lincoln or a big Chrysler. Before Arthurine could get a good look at it, Wind Bag waved at her and Arthurine ducked inside the kitchen, pretending not to notice her. There was nothing Arthurine despised more than a gossip.

Arthurine opened the oven door and looked at the potpies inside. She generally cooked things for the children which took a short time, like frozen dinners or canned green beans that tasted like tin and were the bland color of janitors' uniforms. "Go to hell, you old Wind Bag!" Arthurine told the potpies, poking at them with a fork. Yellow gravy spurted from the holes in the crust.

Her stomach abruptly tied itself into a knot. She had a feeling something bad was about to happen, or was happening already, maybe a mile away. Then the feeling of foreboding receded. She banged the oven shut and rattled around in the silverware drawer, forgot what she was searching for, and looked back out the window.

Wind Bag had crept along the side of her house and was squatting only ten feet away, poking around in the dirt with her rake and lopping off elephant ear plants with a long kitchen knife. Sophie Pulley was a half-bald henna-haired woman who bought dirt at the store to plant her lantana in. She said that the real soil had too much clay in it. Beside Wind Bag, a yellow lantana backed against the Pulley house on a thin stretch of dirt.

The lantana reminded Arthurine of a man in a movie trying to cling to a window ledge to keep from plummeting off a skyscraper after he'd changed his mind about committing suicide. Wind Bag turned around and looked up toward Arthurine's window. Arthurine backed away, but not in time—Wind Bag's voice followed her into the kitchen.

"You won't guess what little Miss Oaks said to that poor young Mr. Oaks this morning! You could hear her clear 'cross the street. She yelled out, 'Why don't you pick up some groceries for once in your life today on the way home so you don't starve to death, you dumb you-know-what sucker!' " Wind Bag could not bring herself to say the words, but Arthurine noted that Wind Bag paused for a moment as if savoring the recollection of them. "He kept walking with his back to her like he hadn't heard a thing. So she said, twice, 'You big ugly fat loud lousy bastard! You big ugly fat loud lousy bastard!' He still didn't answer her, but he kind of bent to the side like he'd been hit with a stone."

Wind Bag paused to see if Arthurine would respond, and then added: "She's got that man fetching and carrying for her, he pretends he don't even notice she has a mouth on her big as a kitchen sink. Some young men are that way nowadays, they put up with anything from a woman. She's at him all hours, in broad daylight for everyone and their uncle to see, and he just bows and scrapes and smiles this sad smile. Don't that take the cake?"

"Don't that take the cake?" Arthurine mimicked, too low for Wind Bag to hear. Wind Bag was always plotting to tempt Arthurine into a conversation. When Wind Bag had first moved to New Orleans from Lafayette, she had acted friendly and trapped Arthurine into letting her up on the porch to chat. For weeks afterward they had sat together, laughing at each other's jokes and confirming each other's opinions. But the last time they had talked on the porch had been Wind Bag's sixtieth birthday one month before. Arthurine had bought Wind Bag a vanilla ice cream cake and they had enjoyed themselves gabbing and washing down the cake with Constant Comment.

Wind Bag had opened the conversation with "What's the worst thing you ever did?" This was exactly the sneaky kind of move Wind Bag might make, ask you an irresistible question in order to find out everything about you.

When they both had begun their third pieces of cake, Arthurine talked about her daughter, Gert, and Stanley's father, Ross Wilkes. It was understood that Arthurine spoke in confidence.

Three days later, Arthurine caught Wind Bag badmouthing her to the Tulane student, Mr. Oaks, who had moved onto the block only a little while before with a scary-looking little wife who dressed in beige suits and gold earrings and carried a briefcase.

"It's a tragedy is what it is." Wind Bag had stood in the street talking at him. She was wearing a three-dollar housedress and yellow slippers with tiger heads over the toes. Her thin hair stood up in wisps on her head, and it did not occur to her what a sight she presented to Mr. Oaks. "It's terrible to consider what that boy's up against, with a father like that, who'd beat up his own wife and baby and not come home for days at a stretch. He hasn't even seen the boy in years, the mother's been running around with another man named Buddy for some time, and now all of a sudden the father comes back from the dead and telephones her to say that he's claiming the boy. That's why he's with his grandmother—to keep his whereabouts secret. And meanwhile, he must just go on thinking he's not wanted, who knows what the boy's been told—"

"What's he care about my business!" Arthurine had crept up behind Mr. Oaks, scaring him half to death. "You keep your old wind bag tied up!"

When Arthurine peeked out the kitchen window, she saw Wind Bag chopping pink camellias from a bush with the kitchen knife, and signaling to Netta to take some of the flowers inside. Wind Bag looked dangerous, the knife's honed edge glinting in her hand, and a three-pronged rake's pointy metal teeth shimmering in the grass beside her. Netta approached, lifted the rake, and sunk its long teeth into the dirt with a satisfied expression, as if the rake were a dangerous animal she was privileged to handle. Then she grabbed Wind Bag's camellias, bruising the petals by clutching at them while the boys hovered around her.

The three children burst through the screen door and Netta dumped the camellias onto the table.

"Well, look what the old battle-ax sent in!" Arthurine said to Netta, winking at her. Netta grinned appreciatively.

"When's food?" said Stanley, looking toward the oven.

"When I tell you to eat it," said Arthurine. "Get outside and air out your pants."

Stanley hooted and raced out the door.

"Eat a banana and go to Atlanna," Netta answered, running after Stanley. Roy followed, shooting at them with a plastic machine gun that purred when he pulled the trigger.

"Atom bomb!" Netta yelled, throwing a brick into the air. When the brick hit the road, all of the children fell down and played dead on the sidewalk.

• • •

He had eyes the color of emeralds, and the tires on his car were new and black as onyx. He drove a rented 1964 gold Chrysler New Yorker, which he pretended to himself that he owned. The Chrysler was so enormous that it had to straddle both lanes of the street before pulling alongside the curb opposite the house.

"I don't care whether you want to eat it or not. Just eat it," Arthurine was telling Netta.

Stanley caved in the top of his chicken potpie and looked out the kitchen window to see what Roy was staring at. Stanley watched a tall man dressed in a white shirt and brown pants get out of a golden car. Wind Bag's spotted dog ran down the street barking at him. The man held out his hand for the dog to smell, like someone who wanted people to think he knew dogs and was not afraid of them. Wind Bag's dog wagged its tail, and the man stroked its head and walked slowly toward the house. After a few steps, he ignored the dog.

"At Immaculate," said Netta, "if you go into the bathroom during recess and cut off the light and then turn around three times and look in the mirror, you'll see the Bloody Mary. That's how come the girls were scared to pee in the school bathroom."

Arthurine raised her eyebrows.

"That man's headed this way," said Roy. "He just stepped out that big gold car over there and now he's coming up the walk."

Arthurine went to the front hall. She looked through the screen door, and her heart stopped when she saw the man approaching her porch. Arthurine latched the door. She had not laid eyes on Ross Wilkes in years, but she recognized him by his smell. Not the smell of cigarettes, but the odor of fresh tobacco. Arthurine had seen him last at Gert's wedding in Raleigh, North Carolina, where Wilkes came from. As Arthurine watched Stanley's father approach, North Carolina came back to her: there was tobacco strewn everywhere. People even mulched their gardens with it. She had gotten sick to her stomach and developed a headache before the wedding started.

The children pushed their noses against the screen door.

Wilkes rose slowly onto the porch, bending his knees just slightly as he came up the steps, in the way of tall men. His brown shoes made a hollow sound on the porch. The soles were long and slender, and the shoe shadows under them shrank and lengthened with the rise and fall of his feet. Wilkes's tie was loosened at the neck and hung like a rumpled tobacco leaf. He carried a pin-striped suit jacket folded over his arm, and he smiled a thin-lipped salesman's smile beneath a brown homburg hat, which he did not remove.

"Which one of them bows is mine?" Wilkes said, pointing down at Roy and Stanley through the screen door.

"None of them," said Arthurine. "I'm babysitting my neighbor's children, Mr. Wilkes." He bent down and looked at her through the wire mesh.

"You Stanley's daddy, right?" Netta said, pushing in front of the boys.

"That's right, Lady Bug," Wilkes told her. "How'd you get so smart?" He looked up at Arthurine. "Cain't you get your grandma to lemme in?" He leaned forward, and his knee jostled two quart-sized Coca-Cola bottles lined up outside the door. The bottles clinked and tumbled and rolled across the porch. The children noted with interest that neither adult moved to retrieve them.

"I think you should hightail it out of here," said Arthurine. "You don't have any business coming here."

"That's my business," said Wilkes, pointing not at his own son, but at Roy, whom Wilkes thought might belong to him.

"Why that's nothing but Roy!" said Stanley, suddenly interested. "I'm the one is Stanley."

"You hush up," said Arthurine. Over Wilkes's shoulder, she could see Wind Bag standing on the sidewalk with her kitchen knife and rake, staring at all of them. As Arthurine leaned to the side and frowned to make Wind Bag leave, Netta unhitched the latch to the screen door.

Wilkes jerked it open and put his foot over Arthurine's threshold.

"You aren't going to tell a man he cain't see his own little child are you?" Wilkes continued, sliding his foot a little farther so that it blended with the cool brown shadows inside the hallway.

"I never heard these past few years that you cared that much about seeing him," said Arthurine. The way Arthurine pushed her weight between Wilkes and the children reminded him of an old goose defending her eggs. He stopped edging forward, took off his hat, and wiped his forehead on his sleeve.

"I din't mean to cause you no kind of trouble," he said. "Maybe if I just sat down here on the front steps you wouldn't refuse a man a cool glass of ice tea on a hot day like this." Wilkes put his hat back on, slipped his foot from the door, walked backward across the porch, and sat down on the top step. "You could fry an egg on the sidewalk on a day like this."

Arthurine hesitated. "All right," she said. "Don't come any farther than that and I'll ask Netta to get you some tea."

Before Arthurine had finished speaking, Netta sprang from the screen door and ran into the kitchen. A minute later, she came back giggling and carrying a glass of iced tea. Arthurine noted to herself that Netta, who had always been a tomboy, was acting peculiarly girlish.

"Here you go," said Arthurine, turning to Roy. "You carry this out to Mr. Wilkes." Stanley watched Roy take the glass and hold it in front of him like an altar boy. Arthurine pushed open the screen door, and Stanley followed Roy to the end of the porch.

"Thank *you,*" Wilkes said politely, taking the tea. Then he looked across the street and shaded his eyes like a sailor studying the movement of an ocean animal across a seascape.

"See that car?" said Wilkes, pointing to the Chrysler. "I've driven that car all over the country. I been to Tinnisee and Missippi and Laoosiana and Florda in it. I like a big old kind of car like that because when you start it up, it don't cry like those whiny little cars they make now. When I start up that car, it sounds like this: *B'lum, B'lum B'lum Badadum Blooroom!*"

The boys' mouths dropped open, and they looked at the Chrysler. Wilkes sipped his tea as if he were unaware of their interest. Wind Bag's liver-spotted dog moved in a bowlegged strut up to the porch and glowered at Wilkes.

He extended a long arm and tickled the dog on the head. The dog settled down on the bottom step.

"You bows good with animals?" Wilkes asked Stanley. "Us Wilkeses always had a way with animals." Stanley nodded. Wilkes looked back in the direction of the car.

"One day I saw an ad in the paper: 1964 Chrysler New Yorker, it said. Nine hundred ninety-nine dollars. Good condition, it said. I was in Mimphis at the time, and driving a rented little nothing of a car, so I went to have a look. The minute I laid eyes on that New Yorker, I knew I might never meet another car like it. It had power windows. You know, push-button windows. You press a lever and the window goes *ZZZZmmmm.*"

"*ZZZZmmmm,*" said Stanley and Roy.

Wilkes nodded. "This is the best ice tea I ever had," he said, sipping from his glass. "And the car had automatic door locks," he continued. "They go down when you hit a button in the front, like ghosts is pressing on them. A real nice radio and a long antenna that'll get you Nashville stations all the way in Pensacola. Air conditioning, wide seats you can sit back in, power steering, big American V-8. I told Mr. Conrad, the man who owned it, nice fella, I'd give him six sixty-six for it. But he said no, that was the devil's number and it was nine hundred ninety-nine or nothing. So I gave him ten one-hundred-dollar bills and he gave me exactly ten dimes back.

"Well, I guess I better be going now," Wilkes said, swallowing the last mouthful of tea. He placed the glass on the porch, and turned to Stanley. "You tell the ladies thank you kindly." Stanley barely listened as the screen door clapped behind him and his grandmother approached with Netta. He watched Wilkes retreat down the steps and across the street to the car.

"You can stay right here on the porch!" Arthurine called out, but Stanley was already staggering like a man in a trance, down the stairs to the sidewalk. Arthurine stood suspended for a moment as Wilkes swung the car around in a graceful U-turn and kissed the curb with his tires. Before she could move, Wilkes was sliding across the car seat and opening the door and grabbing Stanley by his little arm.

"Let go of him!" Arthurine cried, Roy and Netta parting in front of her and swirling around her like spots of light under water. The Chrysler's door began to inch closed. Wind Bag moved in a half circle around Arthurine's outer line of vision. Arthurine rushed down the steps and across the sidewalk, but when she reached the car, only Stanley's ankle and foot remained unswallowed. Arthurine grabbed for his shoe, but it came off in her hand. She grasped his ankle.

"You skunk!" Arthurine yelled through the crack in the car door. "Let go of Stanley!"

"He's mine. He belongs to me," Wilkes answered.

Netta and Roy watched from the porch, seemingly paralyzed with interest. They saw Stanley's foot pulled out of the car and then yanked back in again. They watched Wilkes in the driver's seat, his right arm tightening around Stanley's chest, just under his armpits. They stood motionless when Wilkes pulled Stanley in one quick jerk so that he landed on his father's lap. The door slammed, and the automatic locks popped down simultaneously on all four doors.

"Nooooo!" Stanley's voice sailed from the car. The two children on the porch jumped as if they were fish in the same pool and someone had just thrown a stone into its center. They darted toward the screen door and each picked up a Coke bottle. Behind them they heard the *Badadadoom* of the car. They turned and threw the bottles in the direction of the Chrysler. For a moment Arthurine saw the bottles suspended in perfect arcs of light that reminded her of the shoulders of angels. Then they bounced off the car hood and shattered on the ground.

Wind Bag sprang from behind the car, looking murderous, the kitchen knife raised in her hand. She stabbed at a front tire's sidewall. The dalmatian heaved itself in a whirl of spots against the far window, trying to bite Wilkes through the glass. Wind Bag's kitchen knife snapped at the point and clattered to the pavement. Arthurine clutched a windshield wiper, pressing her upper body against the hood, and heard the car make a quiet noise like a man clearing his throat. It crept slowly forward and Arthurine slipped backward onto the sidewalk.

Then words leapt out of Arthurine's mouth: "Help me, Sophie! I'm losing him! Where's my girl? Why isn't Gertie here? I'm not ready to lose him, Sophie! I hardly know who he is yet!"

Beside her, Wind Bag was bent over, placing an object in the back wheel's path. Arthurine could not tell if she had been heard. Wind Bag jumped back from the car, watching the wheel. A moment later, there were sounds of metal rasping the pavement, the creaking of rubber, and a whoosh of air.

Netta and Roy shouted, "The tire! The tire!"

The back tire's treads rolled over the teeth of Wind Bag's three-pronged rake. The rake gripped the black rubber. Its wooden handle twisted upward with the turning wheel and battered the underbelly of the car. The Chrysler lurched away from the curb, listing to the side.

As Wilkes nosed the car down Prytania Street, the rake rose and fell. Its handle splintered and clattered against the axle, and then turned outward like the slow tail of a patient, iron-jawed animal. The car crept around the corner in the direction of Saint Charles Avenue as Arthurine, Wind Bag, and the children clustered after. The dog hurled itself against Wilkes's window, landed on its back, and stood up with a stunned expression. The rake circled inward, bowed, and then straightened with a terrible rattle. The front hubcap sank deeply into its flat tire. The Chrysler stopped dead still.

When Wilkes swung open his door and jumped onto the pavement, he knocked off his brown homburg hat. It rolled crazily down the street as he loped in an awkward, gangly run toward Saint Charles. Wind Bag's liver-spotted dalmatian snarled and barked after Wilkes, pursuing him joyfully for half a block, then raced back down the road in the direction of the Chrysler. The dog grabbed Wilkes's hat in its teeth, shook it several times, and ran with it toward the Pulley house. Stanley stepped down from the car and walked shaky-legged toward Arthurine, with a half-astonished, half-pleased expression. Beside him the car lay like a great beached animal, sparkling under the glittering sun.

HOT SPRINGS

MRS. HOPE DOHERTY sat in the front seat, tugging at her dress and fanning herself and fiddling with the air-conditioning levers and talking and talking.

"Y'all will like California. You got to visit the parks they have over there. I've seen all the national parks out West. Yosemite, Sequoia, Yellowstone, the Grand Canyon, Death Valley. Once I went to visit the boiling mud pots, and a man standing only six feet away from me slips down the bank and falls right into them! The mud just steamed and boiled over him and he sank, they never found the body or nothing. But Hot Springs is different. The springs are natural but they're kind of domesticated, know what I'm saying? They're all surrounded by walkways and big hotels."

"It's coming up, Mama," Stanley said, peering over the front seat between Mrs. Doherty and his mother.

"We should be seeing that turn again any minute, Gertie," Mrs. Doherty confirmed.

Gert looked at her son in the rearview mirror; he had placed his baseball cap in the lap of his overalls, and his hair was sticking straight up like orange cat fur. He had a dirt beard, and the white sections of his cap were soiled to a rust red.

"Stanley, you look a mess," Gert told her son.

Stanley smiled in reply and delicately placed his hat back onto his head as he looked at his mother's black hair; it lay every which way on her head like grass trampled by a wild animal.

Gert continued, "Anyone would believe we left you to sleep outside on the ground. I swear, Hope, all we did this morning was walk from the hotel to the car. You'd think we dressed him in dirty clothes every morning." Gert suddenly remembered Stanley had fallen asleep in his overalls the night before and *was* wearing dirty clothes.

"Gert, do you see that sign there?" Mrs. Doherty cried out. Gert forgot to turn on the blinker and veered sharply to the left. She was having trouble paying attention to her driving. She had missed the turnoff to Hot Springs twice, because whenever Mrs. Doherty stopped talking, Gert heard Buddy Shipley's voice fighting against hers in last night's argument.

"I thought you were going to do me up these shoes, Gertie." The shoes snuggled against each other in his hand like two brown piglets.

"And what's wrong with them?"

Buddy held them up higher.

"Well, I'm sorry, they just wouldn't come clean and I ran out of polish a week ago."

"My mother blacked my daddy's shoes every night."

"Well, I'm not your mother. Your mother's another lady. She lives in another state. I'm your wife. You only have one mama and nobody's spoiled enough to need two."

Buddy had looked at Gert so forlornly, sitting down on the bed and depositing the empty shoes beside his narrow, boyish feet, that Gert had slammed the door and walked out to buy shoe polish.

"Gert, you can pull right over here and hook around to the left. There's a parking space to the side of that bank there."

It had been Mrs. Doherty's idea to spring Gert and Stanley from Little Rock for the day to go to Hot Springs. They had taken Mrs. Doherty's car, a Plymouth with low fins and a push-button gearshift, and she was letting Gert drive to cheer her up.

Gert steered toward the curb, and pushed a button on the dashboard. The windshield wipers turned on. "Wrong gear," she said gaily, turning the wipers off and pushing another button. This time the car made a gentle sound like a refrigerator motor, and rolled backward in one deft motion onto its rectangle of asphalt.

"Well, now, I think I'll hire you as my chauffeur," said Mrs. Doherty, unbuckling her seat belt. "There's a hot water fountain on that big hill, but you don't want to climb all the way up there, it's not worth all that huffing and puffing on a hot day. There's a nice little walkway with water pools right up the street there that are every bit as good. I know Stanley will love Hot Springs." She turned around in her seat. "After we go see the spring we'll drive up the road to the I.Q. Zoo where chickens play the piano and a rabbit will take your photograph. They use some special way to teach animals there to do all kinds of things that lots of people can't learn. Then we'll go to the Alligator Farm and eat barbecue for dinner at Stubby's. You'll like that, won't you, honey?"

Stanley thought he might.

Gert reached behind the seat for her purse. "That sound OK to you, hun?"

"Yep."

Gert fumbled inside her purse for her compact, frowned into it, withdrew mascara, eye shadow, and lipstick, and painted on the face she had seen in *Seventeen* two weeks before and had been wearing since: green eyelids whiskered with mascara, tabby-orange rouge, and a thin, upturned mouth.

Gert held her face perfectly still and leaned forward to look in the rearview mirror. "It'll have to do," she said, sitting back down. She piled her makeup into the purse and, resting her hands on the steering wheel, told Mrs. Doherty, "I never thought I'd let him skip school. Aren't we wicked?"

"You like school?" Mrs. Doherty asked Stanley, fishing for her own purse. Mrs. Doherty was a large-boned lady with a long nose that dipped and widened at the end like a cow's. She was wearing a spotted black and white dress and was the first woman Stanley had seen close up who did not use lipstick. Her lips were wide and pale. She rented a room in the Little Colonel Hotel on a monthly basis, and when Stanley walked home from school, he usually went straight upstairs to Mrs. Doherty's, where he would find his mother whooping and laughing and talking in a loud voice alternating with furtive whispers.

"Nope," Stanley answered.

"Well, it's a good thing you aren't there then." Mrs. Doherty laughed. Mrs. Doherty often said she took great pleasure in the fact that she had never finished high school but had grown rich selling useless, outlandish clothes to college girls and bored society wives. She owned a clothing store called Paraphernalia two blocks from the hotel.

Mrs. Doherty and Gert slid out of their seats, opened the back doors, and tugged at the plastic jugs and watercoolers piled in a barricade on either side of Stanley. When Stanley had crawled out of the car, Mrs. Doherty and Gert gently shut the Plymouth's doors and walked toward the hill.

Mrs. Doherty insisted on taking an extra watercooler from Gert. "You're thin as a stick, gimme that thing." Stanley unhooked himself from the cooler as his mother let go of it, and he resettled his hand in hers.

"You know that awful sweater I showed you?" Mrs. Doherty continued. "Looked like it was made out of dyed purple chicken feathers? Mrs. La-De-Da Rollins bought it. 'That sweater is you,' I told her."

Gert answered, "They can't get him to read, but I couldn't read that well when I was seven either. He's only in second grade! And then he switched schools so many times. I thought he should repeat first grade so he wouldn't always be behind everyone else, but Buddy said you can't tie a boy to your apron strings. So then I kept telling Buddy that as long as we were in Little Rock we should at least put Stanley in Our Lady, where he'd get more attention, but Buddy has this thing about the pope an' all. Well, Stanley will come along."

Buddy Shipley rarely spoke directly to Stanley, but Stanley had been relieved to hear him say that no kid of his girlfriend's was going to any Catholic school. Stanley had seen the pale, plaid-uniformed children lining up noiselessly outside Our Lady.

"I told Buddy all these moves aren't good for a little boy, and that maybe it's just as well he lost his job, that maybe he could find some other work and we could settle down a while. Whoosh! You should see the look Buddy gave me. He has his mind set on California."

After Buddy Shipley had been laid off from his job as an itinerant manager for the Little Colonel Hotel chain, he awoke one midnight in early May and reflected on the first dream he ever remembered remembering. Buddy and Gert and her son, Stanley, were riding in Buddy's old green convertible across a desert. Ahead of them, a road stretched and undulated like an electric eel. When Buddy looked carefully at the asphalt, he saw that the road was actually a bright, inky canal of water, and that the car was moving through it, wheelless, like a boat. The desert deepened in color and sprang up in front of Buddy and extended into an enormous arch. He recognized the arch as a picture of the Golden Gate Bridge he had seen in a *Life* in the hotel lobby.

All the rest of May, Buddy talked about the dream to Gert as if it were more real to him than his own family. He cut out the magazine picture and stuck it to the bathroom mirror. Buddy told Gert that everyone he knew who was anybody had moved to California. He said that by the year 2000, half of California would be southerners. San Francisco would be as flashy as Dallas.

He wrote an old navy friend in San Diego, who sent a letter saying that he could get Buddy a modest job as an undermanager in a fancy hotel, to commence in July. Gert understood that nothing she could do would prevent Buddy from leaving Arkansas for California. When she saw the state of California on the map, she thought it looked like a badly shaped piecrust, but finally she had given in. California was where men moved when they grew discontent with what they were, and although Gert worried about uprooting Stanley again, she felt the force of history was against her.

Stanley had moved five times in three years, as Buddy Shipley was transferred from one Little Colonel Hotel to another. Stanley had resided in Memphis long enough to call it Mimphis, had spoken with a subdued, mumbling drawl in Georgia and a rubbery twang when he lived in Montgomery, and immediately had mastered a springy nasal accent in Little Rock. Some mornings when he woke up he did not know which manner of speech, accompanied by its own nuances of personality, would sail from his mouth when he dared to open it. When Mrs. Doherty talked in her soft New Orleans accent, Stanley felt himself swaying back and forth, as if cradled by swishing bathtub water. He vaguely recalled a time when his mother had talked the same way, before her accent had been filed down and rubbed smooth by constant moving. When Buddy had transferred to the Little Colonel in Miami, right before the move to Little Rock, Stanley had begun to speak with a foreign inflection, like the Finnish man who permanently rented the General Robert E. Lee suite in the left wing.

Stanley could not get past the *y* in his first name when Gert tried to show her son how to write Stanley Wilkes (she alternately mentioned as possible last names Shipley, and her maiden name, Ray, and even her mother's maiden name, Beaulieu, but she never showed Stanley any of these others on paper). Stanley would stare distrustfully at the little *y* when he saw what a shady kind of vowel it was, capable of a forceful twangy sound but silent in *Stanley*. He had heard his name pronounced "Stayinly" in Arkansas and "Stanluh" in Georgia, and listened to citified Miami people say "Stan*lee*," as if only the last part of his name were meaningful. Inwardly he felt too indefinite and fragile to print his signature with a green and gold Dixon Ticonderoga pencil.

The gaunt man with the twisted leg was sitting so close to the spring that he seemed to be guarding it. But his face lit up when he saw Stanley, and he said, "Go ahayed and touch it and see how hawt it is." The man wore a visored red cap and had a toothless, lipless face that collapsed over his chin, and large ears that leaned forward, cupping the air. He rolled up his pants leg and showed Stanley the scar of a bullet wound gotten in World War I, and he listened politely as Mrs. Doherty told him the early history of Hot Springs while Gert sat staring vacantly in front of her, or glaring into her compact, or pushing back her cuticles.

As Stanley kneeled down to stick his hand in the bubbling water, Mrs. Doherty was saying, ". . . they came from everywhere in the old days during the wunner to take a cure and stayed in those hotels there, and you had to reserve a room to take a bath, and you could sit in the tub all day until you felt you were pure steam, just all whispery and vapory like a ghost. Once I fainted . . ."

Stanley dipped his fingertip in the water and then

plunged in his hand. "Man, it's hawt!" Stanley shrieked, jerking back his arm and then sticking it in again.

The man finally stood, winking at Stanley and tipping his cap at Mrs. Doherty, and limped down the wide path. Stanley circled Mrs. Doherty and limped after him, surveying the ground for rare or unusually colorful or root beer bottle caps.

Gert watched Mrs. Doherty fold in three places in order to stoop and submerge a jug in the spring. When she had finished filling the fourth jug, Mrs. Doherty said, "You're not really supposed to do this here, you're supposed to use the hot water fountain, but who cares?"

"You know," said Gert, "now he's not working anymore, he's stopped calling me his wife in front of people. He introduces us as 'my girlfriend Gertie and her son.' Before that, we were always planning to marry and Buddy promised to adopt Stanley and everything. But somehow we never got around to it, with all those moves. He hardly takes any interest in me and Stanley anymore. All he talks about nowadays is California. And Unemployment. You know he doesn't believe in Unemployment. So after he comes back from standing in line all day, he goes on and on telling me, 'I'm different, I earned it, I've been putting my money into the till. Those other guys are freeloading off the government, they've been standing on that line most of their lives, but I've been working my whole life and I'm only taking back a few months what I've been putting in all those years.' "

"Men get so hard to take when they can't work," Mrs. Doherty said, screwing the last watercooler shut. "You have to be an angel to put up with them. You should have seen him when I asked if you could work at the Paraphernalia. He stumped around the room like the carpets was full of bugs. He sure don't like me very much."

"That's not so, Hope. He doesn't have a thing against you, it's just that he doesn't like anybody at all anymore."

"I never did meet a husband who felt comfortable around me." Mrs. Doherty laughed, unfolding herself and standing up. Mrs. Doherty had a stream of boyfriends, but her own husband had left her twenty years ago, after three days of marriage. She had once said that he took everything when he left, even her wedding ring off the sink, and her bridal gown with white high heels. Gert had wondered what he would do with the dress—sell it? Use it for his next wife? Sleep beside it? Gert pictured a pale wedding gown lying specterlike on a dark bed next to a sleeping man.

"You know, Buddy would never run off and quit us. But sometimes it's, well, like everybody rotates around him, and he hardly notices me. But I just wouldn't have the courage to leave if things got bad. I been there once before, I can't even fall asleep at night if I'm left alone. But things won't get that bad. Buddy's a real find, I should know after Ross Wilkes—Buddy doesn't drink or get rough or play around or anything. And now that Ross has tracked us down again and keeps frightening Stanley with those phone calls, it's probably just as well we're moving again. But I swear it hardly seems to matter to Buddy if we tag along. Oh Jesus, I don't know what I'm talking about."

"Looks like Stanley's going to have to help us carry these jugs." Mrs. Doherty placed the smaller ones in the cooler. "Well, you know how some men are? Living in the same house with you but not even there?"

Gert turned with wide eyes to Mrs. Doherty.

"They don't have to get up and leave you, because they're already gone."

Gert jumped up. "Where's Stanley?" The women looked around them, and then down the walkway, where they saw Stanley creeping behind the man who had been sitting by the spring.

"Stan-uh-lee!" Mrs. Doherty cupped her lips and hollered. Stanley galloped back, his overall pockets jingling with bottle caps.

At the I.Q. Zoo, after Stanley played tic-tac-toe with a chicken and lost, he and his mother and Mrs. Doherty followed a family with an uncountable number of children into a dark room. The animal trainer took out a group of red, blue, and yellow macaws and directed them to a row of perches. Gert found herself watching the large family instead of the birds. There were over ten children, almost all boys, and a mother who looked twelve months pregnant holding a baby, and a lank man with a long face clutching two boys in one hand and a girl in the other. A row of boys lined up in front of him. They had various colors of hair, butterscotch and black and a brown midway in between, and reminded Gert of a crossbred litter of puppies. They pushed against one another to see the birds. One macaw, whom the trainer had told to roller-skate, was clutching two wheeled weights in his claws and lifting them one at a time in determined steps across the stage.

The pregnant woman tilted forward and whispered to the man, "Hun, it's so hot in here. I don't feel good at all."

But the man was mesmerized by a parrot strutting forward to shoot off a toy cannon. "It won't take long," he answered, looking down at the boys. "We paid so much, we better see it on out."

The woman stepped back and shifted her baby to her other arm.

Stanley jumped when the cannon went HUCK! and shot a ball into the crowd.

He worked his way through the group of boys by the stage to get a closer look at the razorback hog that paraded before them, waiting for directions. The boys moved over without noticing Stanley, their eyes fixed on the hog as it pushed a coal cart along a miniature railroad track.

"Hun, please, I really don't feel well." Stanley saw the boys' mother looking meaningfully at her husband. "I'm gonna take R.E. and go out and see if I can find a Coke somewhere."

The man let go of the little girl, then pulled a dollar bill out of his pocket and gave it to his wife. "OK, baby, I'll bring Penny and the boys out later myself and we'll look around for you." His wife backtracked across the room and went out the door, hoisting the baby to her shoulder.

The man reached down and took Stanley by the hand. At first Stanley was surprised, but then he let his hand stay in the long, moist fingers of the man. Stanley looked at his mother and Mrs. Doherty standing on the left side of the stage, but they did not seem to notice.

For the rest of the show, he clung to the man from one dark room to the other as they watched ducks play the banjo and chickens walk tightropes. When the show was over, Stanley ambled through the I.Q. Zoo's souvenir store still holding on to the man, who followed his string of children past Mrs. Doherty and Gert and the other family, out into the hot air of the street.

Gert looked at postcards while Mrs. Doherty paid the cashier to have her picture taken by a rabbit. The cashier focused a box camera on Mrs. Doherty, and a black and white rabbit walked out of a cage and perched on a second camera connected to the first, aiming it at Mrs. Doherty's profile. He raised his paw and pressed a lever and the first camera let out a burst of light. The cashier pulled a square of film out of the camera, watched the rabbit climb back in his cage, and then peeled a strip of plastic off the film and handed the photograph to Mrs. Doherty.

"Look here, Gert," Mrs. Doherty called out. "The rabbit will take a picture of you getting your picture taken by a rabbit. We just have to do one all together."

Gert examined the photograph Mrs. Doherty held up in front of the postcards. "Oh, that's funny. Stanley, we've got to do that too." Gert looked around but saw only a couple with three yellow-haired children lining up in front of the camera and no Stanley.

"Did Stanley come out of the room with us, Hope?" Gert walked through the store into the animal rooms, with visions of Stanley crying in some dark corner, lost. The cashier followed behind with Mrs. Doherty, turning on the lights. "He's not here!"

Gert slipped back through the store and rushed to the front door of the I.Q. Zoo. Stanley was nowhere in sight. She turned to the cashier and said, "Is there some door back here he could have gone out, or someplace he could be hiding?"

"No, there's no doors. Why would he be hiding?" The cashier focused on Gert with an accusatory expression.

Mrs. Doherty looked outside a second time. "There he is, right there."

Gert saw the pregnant woman walking toward the I.Q. Zoo and leading Stanley by the hand.

"Is he yours?" she called out. "My husband didn't realize he had the wrong little boy." The woman laughed. "He thought it was just another one of ours. We would have drove off if my girl Penny hadn't asked about him."

Mrs. Doherty answered with a bellowing laugh.

"Don't that beat all," said the woman. "As if we don't have too many already." Stanley let go of her hand and moved shyly over to Gert, pulling down his cap and looking into his pocket.

"Well, thanks for bringing him back," said Gert. She hoped she sounded calm and lighthearted like the woman, and that her voice did not betray the terror and hysteria and relief whirling inside her.

"You're welcome to some of our other ones too," said the woman as she walked away. "Take your pick."

Stanley saw four boys staring at him out of the windows of a station wagon while the man, who sat in the driver's seat, looked directly ahead as if he did not want to be noticed. Stanley stepped behind Mrs. Doherty until the car drove away. When it passed them, the woman leaned in front of her husband, pressing on the steering wheel so that the car honked three times to Stanley's mother and Mrs. Doherty.

Gert led Stanley back inside and he sat with his mother and Mrs. Doherty in front of the camera, posing for the rabbit. While Mrs. Doherty paid for the photograph, Gert looked through the postcards of Hot Springs. She picked out ten of them, saw that no one was paying attention to her, and slipped the postcards into her purse. Gert was surprised at herself, but then she also felt a pleasant spitefulness toward Hot Springs.

As she walked toward the exit, her purse seemed heavier and fuller.

"Whoosh," Mrs. Doherty said, once they were all three safely outside. "What a long day. I think we're going to have to skip the Alligator Farm for now and go right to Stubby's."

Gert turned toward her son. "You feel like eating, honey?"

Stanley nodded, and looked at the photograph in his hand: a red-haired boy stared back at him, wedged between his mother and Mrs. Doherty. Mrs. Doherty's head was turned toward the rabbit, her mouth open in mock surprise as the rabbit eyed her, seeming to ready the camera. Stanley's mother was looking down at the red-haired boy, with her hands grasping his shoulders like clothespins, as if she were afraid the next wind would blow him loose and carry him upward into the air.

BOOKS

WHENEVER Stanley tried to read, the words crowded together and flipped over like fish swimming upstream, backward across the paper. Threats, coaxing, deprivation, and elaborate forms of humiliation would not move him to read aloud. Mrs. Heffernan, his third grade teacher in San Diego, had settled for making Stanley hold his book open while the other children in the slow reading group took their turns.

Mrs. Heffernan was a creative, at times exotic, disciplinarian. She was a large woman, with a large wooden chair parked behind her desk, and if she caught two boys fighting, she would place them together in her chair, and sit down on their legs five or six times. She was prone to fits of rage in which she would lift books high above her head and pound them once, deafeningly, on the edge of her desk, often cracking the bindings and once breaking off a corner of the desk's wooden paneling.

Mrs. Heffernan excused herself to use the bathroom many times a day, always saying that she had to "step out to wash her hands," and leaving the class unattended. At these times she would pull her chair to the front of the room and place on it a green plastic figure of Jiminy Cricket.

"Jiminy is going to watch you while I'm gone," she would tell the class. "And he's going to decide who is bad and who has been good." Sometimes she only pretended to go to the bathroom, and stationed herself outside in the hall, spying on the third grade, testing their trustworthiness.

"Jiminy told me that Maritza Diaz has the filthiest habits of any girl who has ever been in the classroom," Mrs. Heffernan reported at the end of the first school day overseen by Jiminy Cricket. "But Stanley Wilkes is the real winner of the lazy boy contest." Mrs. Heffernan thereafter made similar pronouncements: she often noted that a particular boy or girl had "the dirtiest shirts," "the most unkempt hair," "the ugliest mouth," "the most backward math skills," or "the sloppiest artwork" she had seen in her fifteen years of teaching, as if her career consisted in part of keeping track of records continually being broken. She alternately called Stanley "the saddest reader" and "the least intelligible boy in the class," in reference to his twangy Arkansas accent, which also moved her on several occasions to call him Deputy Dog.

Stanley had not been placed in the slowest of the third grades, however. In 1967, Stanley's school divided children into gifted, average, and special classes. Average children included almost all of the students with Spanish surnames, any black children, and a half dozen white children who, like Stanley, were simply believed to be stupid. The special class was for children classified as "mentally retarded" from all over the city, and also the group in which children who spoke only Spanish were placed. The students in the gifted class ignored the others, and those in the average group generally beat up the gifted students and were thankful for the special class, which they saw as the only limit on their designated ineptitude. Years later, a group of parents would complain about the presence of children with Down's syndrome in the school, and the special class would disappear. After that, the students in the average class felt themselves to be walking the edge of a fathomless ravine.

There were thirty-six students in the average group, but Stanley had only two friends, Joy Revel and Barry Salazar. Joy painted her fingernails red and brushed Dippity-Do in her hair so that it curved around her head and pointed in the back like an inverted volcano. She claimed to be from New Jersey: she talked through her nose, a source of amusement for Mrs. Heffernan, who would pinch her nose between her thumb and forefinger and imitate Joy, sometimes sending the whole class, including Joy, into giggles. Joy also had foreign customs. When she saw a dandelion growing in a crack in the asphalt, she would pick it, flick off the yellow head with her thumbnail, and say as the flower went soaring: "Mrs. Heffernan had a baby and its head popped off!"

Joy's style of refusing to read differed from Stanley's. She pressed the book close to her eyes and picked her way through the sentences like someone walking barefoot on a hot road, skipping right over the new words and the long ones and generally landing on *the, where,* and *what,* shouting them with varying pronunciation. Sometimes as Joy began reading, Mrs. Heffernan would take a tortoiseshell compact from her purse and dab at her face. On one occasion she uprooted several eyebrow hairs with a pair of tweezers. The children around Joy would grow restless with happiness, lose their way in the story, and pinch each other under the reading table. Stanley would draw racing cars on a paper tucked into his reading book, and later show them to Joy. One of these drawings was of a hot rod running over a smirking Jiminy Cricket, and another depicted Joy riding on the hood of a box-shaped racing car, her hair standing straight up with alarm. Joy liked the pictures, and kept them in her desk.

Joy's mother came only once to the playground, on the third day of school. She exerted a kind of reverse magnetism, so that the other mothers backed away from her in startled radii. She was olive skinned, with dyed, whiskey-colored hair, and wore fishnet stockings and a short polka-dot skirt. When she kissed Joy good-bye, Miss Revel handed her a red patent leather purse instead of a lunch box. At lunchtime, Joy revealed that the purse contained a sandwich with the crusts cut off and an olive speared through the center with a toothpick, four carrot sticks, a piece of wedding cake with a plastic bride and groom still standing on it, and four strands of black licorice.

The girls in the average group kept their distance from Joy, and she acted as if this was how she preferred things. Before she wandered into class on the afternoon of the second day of school, girls in the elementary grades had gathered around a single jump rope to sing: "Not last night, but the night before, twenty-five robbers came aknocking at your door. One jumped in!" Joy watched them with her manicured hands on her hips. She selected two of the stupidest, least popular girls to turn her double clothesline and shouted over the playground as she jumped:

> I look around the corner,
> and what do I see?
> A big fat policeman from Tennessee.
> Bet you five dollars
> I can kill that man
> with a gun from my own hand.
> Hands up! Billy billy bill.
> Hands down. Chilly chilly chill.

When the mothers who supervised the playground at recess exchanged looks, Joy began a new song: "Oooooh, Mr. Willoughby, Willoughby, Willoughby—Oooooh, Mr. Willoughby, all night long."

For reasons Stanley did not understand, Joy spent her time with him. Stanley rarely spoke, and when he did, he revealed the incomprehensible Arkansas twang that moved Mrs. Heffernan to call him Deputy Dog. On hot days, Joy would walk around the blacktop with Stanley, talking while he listened. In early fall, the sun would warm the seams of the asphalt to a black putty, and together the two pried up whatever tar they could find, rolling it into an asphalt ball which rapidly grew to the size of a grapefruit, the largest anyone had ever seen. Stanley stored the tar ball in his desk between free periods.

* * *

Barry Salazar read fluently in both Spanish and English and arrived in the third month of third grade without explanation. Stanley and Joy were surveying the outer rim of the blacktop for melted tar when Barry appeared at the school entrance. Stanley picked him out because Mr. Salazar was the only father to appear that year on the playground. A few times, Stanley's mother's boyfriend, Buddy, had taken him to school, but recently Buddy had started working night shifts at the hotel where he served as undermanager. Sometimes he slept at the hotel, and did not come home for days. Stanley had not seen his real father in years, but knew that he called periodically, and that his calls upset Stanley's mother. One time, his mother had set down the phone and told him, "Don't ever go home with anyone but me or Buddy. If a stranger tells you to get in his car, you run, you hear?" Whenever Stanley saw a particularly large or fancy car pull up outside the school, he liked to imagine that a man would lean out and signal to him. Stanley would get close enough to the car to examine it, but stand back far enough to run if anyone did emerge and approach him.

Mr. Salazar carried a black oblong case. He stood near the fence in a bright red shirt, scowling at the school, and Barry stood beside him, also scowling and wearing a red shirt. They both had sun-scorched hair, the color of a dusty car tire. Mr. Salazar signaled in the direction of Joy and Stanley.

Joy turned around to see whom Mr. Salazar was calling, and then said, "Hey, that guy with the suitcase wants us to go over there." She and Stanley stayed where they were.

Mr. Salazar walked toward them, and addressed Stanley. "Son," he said. "Can you tell me where the third grade is?"

Stanley stood still with his mouth open.

"He don't always talk," Joy said, adjusting the asphalt ball to her shoulder.

"I do too tawk," Stanley told Mr. Salazar.

"Who's supposed to be his teacher?" Joy asked.

Mr. Salazar set down his case and opened it, saying, "I know I wrote that somewhere."

Joy looked at the open hand of black hair on Barry's head, passed her eyes down to his waist, and then back to his face, and met his gaze. "XYZ x-amining your zipper," she said.

Barry zipped his fly and flashed her a glittering smile. His front teeth were lined with gold.

Stanley peered over Mr. Salazar's shoulder and saw a trombone lying on moss green velvet inside its case. Mr. Salazar pulled a square of blue paper from a square compartment. There were black dots and sticks, fractions, and a jumble of letters scrawled on the paper. Barry pulled a silver tube with a knob on the end from the case and blew through it. It made a rude noise.

Mr. Salazar took back the mouthpiece and, looking up at Stanley, winked and said, "That's J. J. Johnson speaking to you, son." Mr. Salazar turned the paper upside down and read from it, "Heffernan. Mrs. Heffernan's the teacher."

"That's us, the dumb class!" Joy said.

Mr. Salazar frowned at the air in front of Joy, as if studying her words. He closed his trombone case, studied Stanley for a moment, and said to Barry, "Well, I guess you'll be all right with this guy here." Mr. Salazar absentmindedly passed his hand through Barry's bangs so that the fingers of hair at the top wiggled. Stanley imagined himself as Barry, his own red shirt slightly too big and with one hole in the shoulder, while Mr. Salazar passed a hand through his hair.

Joy led Barry across the blacktop to the classroom where the average class was lining up. On the way, she extracted from him the information that his mother was dead, that he had chipped his front teeth falling onto a freezer at Safeway, and that the teeth had been capped with gold for three months. Stanley alone noticed that Mr. Salazar remained on the blacktop, turning to go only when Barry disappeared behind Joy into the classroom.

Barry carried an oversize cigar box stamped with a label which he later read to Joy and Stanley: MAN TO MAN, SMOKE A ROI-TAN, FOR A TASTE THAT IS BETTER BY FAR. Inside the box were dozens of gold-rimmed, green June beetles Barry had collected from a rotted tree. The box buzzed against his side like a radio.

Generally, new children were introduced to the class after lunch by preordained formula: first name, last name, reading group, school of origin. Barry's arrival, however, was obscured by the advent of a new set of encyclopedias. Mrs. Heffernan directed him into the back row, where Barry chose a desk near Stanley's and Joy's, while two sixth graders unloaded a wooden crate. From the crate they pulled green and ivory volumes embossed with golden letters. Mrs. Heffernan opened some of the books and showed the class dissected frogs, transparent overlays of the human body, erupting volcanoes, planets, a photograph of an astronaut with a rocket ship in the background, and color plates of insects.

She directed the sixth graders to line up the encyclopedias on the highest shelf behind Barry's desk—students who finished their reading assignments early would be allowed to check out one volume at a time. At the moment when the A volume settled into its inaccessible position, Joy and Stanley looked at each other and formed a silent agreement: they didn't want to *read* the encyclopedias; Stanley and Joy wanted to *have* them.

After three weeks, no student had earned the right to check out an encyclopedia. During this period, Barry was not assigned to a reading group, and in his ample free time he established a reputation for scholarly activities never detected by Mrs. Heffernan. He read Spanish-language comic books, translating them to Stanley in whispers, and filled out the pages Joy and Stanley were assigned in their reading workbooks. Barry molded the tar ball into a perfect sphere, and he rubbed down the free school erasers until they were flawless miniature racing cars. He invented the original picture of Mrs. Heffernan, which was passed around the room and embellished with extra breasts and penises, curse words, body hair, and curls of smoke to signify body odor. In a moment of brilliance inspired by boredom, Barry took off his shirt and put it on inside out and backward. He drew a picture of an astronaut circling Saturn in a rocket ship like that in the encyclopedia. Under the picture, he wrote: "The astronaut stood and wiped the sweat from his brow."

Mrs. Heffernan eventually started Barry in the slow group without testing him. He sat between Stanley and Joy, and read fast as a sports announcer in a clipped, Spanish accent, which Mrs. Heffernan mimicked after he had finished. He completed his workbook assignments before anyone else on the first day, but when he raised his hand and asked permission to see the encyclopedias, Mrs. Heffernan did not look up from her desk. However, when Barry walked to the back of the room in an attempt to take an encyclopedia, Mrs. Heffernan said, "Do me the favor of keeping your head on your desk until the end of the period, Barry Salazar, just do me that favor."

At recess, Joy proposed stealing the encyclopedias. She believed Mrs. Heffernan had forgotten about them, but suggested taking just one encyclopedia, and then waiting to see if Mrs. Heffernan noticed. After that, Stanley and Barry and Joy could steal the rest, one by one. Joy wanted the volume with the color plates of insects, but Barry said that a vowel like *I* would soon be missed. There were only five vowels. The three friends decided on the H volume, with its transparent overlays of the dissected man. Barry decided that he should be the one to take the encyclopedia, because he sat closest to the bookshelf. Joy and Stanley would distract Mrs. Heffernan by talking at the pencil sharpener.

Stanley surprised himself by speaking up. "We can hide the book in the cigar bawks," he suggested. He had noted that it would fit perfectly around an encyclopedia. He loved the Roi-Tan box, with its musky odor he associated with Mr. Salazar. Stanley wondered if the encyclopedia would take on the cigar smell.

Barry agreed to transfer the June beetles to a mason jar that night. Joy explained that her mother would become suspicious if she found a book at home—Joy could try hiding it under her bed, but her mother might find the encyclopedia when she vacuumed. When Joy questioned him, Stanley said that he had no space under his bed: his mother's boyfriend, Buddy, had left locked suitcases there. Barry volunteered that he could hide the encyclopedia in plain view in his house: he would camouflage it by placing it on the bookshelf, and his father would never notice.

The next day, Joy accompanied Stanley to the pencil sharpener, but Mrs. Heffernan, who was grading papers at her desk and who had not appeared to be watching, called to Joy that only one person could use the pencil sharpener at a time. Joy sat down, shifted in her seat, raised her hand, shifted some more, and then walked over to Mrs. Heffernan's desk.

"Sit down and raise your hand if you want to ask something," Mrs. Heffernan said.

Joy stayed where she was, fidgeting first on one foot and then the other, until she leaned forward and lied: "Stanley swallowed tar."

Mrs. Heffernan looked up. Stanley returned to his desk.

"He found it on the playground and he swallowed it."

Mrs. Heffernan rose from her chair and walked to Stanley's desk. Joy followed her, and sat down across from Stanley. Mrs. Heffernan bent over with her back to the encyclopedias and, staring directly at him, said confusingly, "Do I see prying eyes? Is this your business? Don't we all have work to do?" Then, addressing Stanley, she said, "When did you swallow the tar?" As Stanley tried to think of an answer, he heard Barry push back his chair. "Answer me! When did you swallow the tar?" She examined Stanley's hands, black on the palms and under his fingernails from collecting asphalt that day for the tar ball.

"Why did you swallow it?" she pressed. "Answer me!"

Stanley was puzzled by Mrs. Heffernan's tone of concern. What would happen if he swallowed a little tar? He put his head on his desk, and looked under his arm behind him: Barry slipped the encyclopedia into the cigar box and closed it.

When Stanley raised his head, he did not understand why Mrs. Heffernan looked so angry, or why she took him by the shoulder and pushed him toward her desk. She pulled out her chair and, setting Jiminy Cricket on it, said, "Jiminy wants all of you to open your desks, and then to sit with your hands folded in front of you. I wonder what he'll discover before I return!"

Mrs. Heffernan led Stanley to the nurse's office. He sat quietly outside while the nurse ran by him to the principal's office, and then ran back to her telephone, and tried unsuccessfully to reach Stanley's mother.

"Sweetheart," the nurse told him as she held her head to the phone, "don't you know that tar is poisonous?" She did not ask if he really had swallowed tar, and he wondered about this. He also pondered the fact that something as untempting and inedible as tar could be poisonous. How did the world know this? Did a man once swallow tar? Who was he and what made him think of doing it?

While Stanley waited, Mrs. Heffernan reappeared, leading Barry into the principal's office and holding Barry's cigar box in one hand. In Barry's free hand, wrapped in a piece of green construction paper, was the tar ball that Stanley and Joy had put together through so many weeks, and which Barry had molded into a perfect sphere. Mrs.

Heffernan directed him to set the tar ball on the principal's desk.

Stanley heard Mrs. Heffernan say, ". . . a miniature thief. He is the most incorrigible, the least teachable boy I have dealt with. He stole it from the new set of encyclopedias—I found it concealed in this filthy box when I asked all the children to open their desks so that I could see if *they* had tar balls." Mrs. Heffernan leaned into view and dropped the Roi-Tan box into the principal's wastebasket. "He can't even read it! I've had to babysit him for a month, when he should be in the special class! A child like this demands more attention than all of the other children put together . . ." The door closed, leaving Barry outside.

Stanley waved, but just as Barry saw him, the nurse exited her office, carrying her purse, and ushered Stanley outside to her car.

"Don't you worry, sweetheart. We're taking you to the emergency ward and your mother's going to meet us there." She made him lie down in the backseat.

Stanley was aware that the school nurse drove too fast: the car rocked around turns and parked with a jerk at the hospital. She led him into a large hallway. When a man in a white uniform laid a hand on Stanley's shoulder, the school nurse said, "I have to stay here to call your mother's house again. Don't be afraid."

The man lifted Stanley up, set him on a wheeled bed, pushed him into an area enclosed by a curtain, and left him there. Stanley peered through the curtain, but could not locate the school nurse.

A hospital nurse pushed another bed alongside the curtain. She did not notice Stanley. Stanley leaned forward and saw her show some papers to an old man lying in the bed.

The old man stared at the papers and cried, "I can't read the words! It doesn't make sense!" The nurse placed the papers on a table between the old man and Stanley, and departed.

"Help me," the old man said. One half of his lip twisted up and the other twisted down. One of his eyes was shut and the other was open. He turned and the open eye fixed on Stanley.

Stanley was afraid the eye would not turn away unless he answered. He leaned forward and said, "This is Stanley Salazar speaking to you, and I can read anythang."

"God help me!" the man answered.

Stanley peered at the papers on the table: he could not make out any of the words. Most of them were small and dark and long, separated by boxes. There were also blue and green words, and a large red word at the bottom.

"It says you are in a hospital."

"God *help* me, Nelly!" the man repeated, his voice louder, his open eye still directed at Stanley. "Nelly nelly!" he screamed.

Stanley drew back, dropping the papers to the floor. He slid down from his bed and ran through the curtain, into the hallway.

"Nelly nelly!" the man hollered after him.

Stanley passed a moaning man wearing a bloodied shirt, and a pale, motionless woman lying on a cot surrounded by doctors. He backed away and turned into another hall, and there was his mother in a yellow dress with her black hair flying.

"Stanley!" she called. He stopped where he was while she rushed to him and knelt down before him. "I was so worried when they called! I thought your father had shown up again and done something terrible, and—what did the doctor do? Have you seen the doctor?"

Stanley shook his head.

"No? Stanley, how long ago did you swallow the tar? Why did you do it, hun? Did you? Did you really eat tar? You didn't eat it at all, did you? Oh Jesus Christ in a bucket, this is funny. Why did they think you swallowed tar? Didn't you tell anyone that you hadn't? Did you eat tar?"

"No," Stanley answered.

Barry did not return to school. The next morning, Joy and Stanley had to stand against the fence before morning recess. They arrived early enough to see Mr. Salazar arguing with Mrs. Heffernan in the classroom before first period. His trombone case bobbed at his side like an angry black dog as he talked. Then he walked out of the room, straight across the playground, oblivious of the four-square and hopscotch grids.

At lunchtime a week later, Stanley loitered at the edge of a jump rope game Joy had started. Joy leapt into the rope, singing:

> Gypsy, Gypsy, Gypsy Rose Lee,
> Where on earth can your old man be?
> He's a lover undercover
> getting down with your mother,
> so spell your name on one foot.
> You got J-O-Y R-E-V-E-L!

All the mothers on the playground seemed to watch Joy and Stanley.

When she finished her turn at the rope, Joy pointed to the mothers and told Stanley, "They're on the lookout for tar balls." Sixth graders had been sent to all the classrooms to give talks on the new school rule against tar balls. Joy crouched and pretended to pry something from the asphalt. One of the mothers drew closer. Behind her, Stanley saw Mr. Salazar leading Barry along the sidewalk bordering the fence.

They were walking fast and the trombone case loped beside them. Barry was dressed in the stiff white shirt, clip-on tie, and gray flannel pants that marked the children who attended the Catholic school four blocks away. When he saw Stanley, Barry grabbed his tie, held it like a noose over his head, and rolled his eyes. Mr. Salazar turned and waved, and father and son continued up the street.

A MEETING ON THE HIGHWAY

ARTHURINE rarely spoke of Grandpa Bubba except in reference to the salmon pink Cadillac he had left her at his death. For a long time, her grandson, Stanley, knew little about him except that he was dead, and that he had not prospered in life. The son of North Texas Methodist farmers who never finished fifth grade, Bubba attended medical school. He witnessed with horror and fascination the brutality and chicanery of the medical profession and, after one year of practice, longed for the powdery pink clay that nestled in the Dust Bowl like rouge in a compact.

Arthurine threatened to leave Bubba if he let her become a farmer's wife. She convinced him that the Veterans Administration, unlike the AMA, had always worked in the service of mankind, and he enlisted. For eight years the family lived on squalid military hospital grounds all over the South, rarely staying longer than nine months in one place. When they moved to New Orleans, a soldier who had returned insane from the South Pacific wrapped his arms in a wrestler's embrace around Bubba's neck. Within a month Bubba died of a rare tropical ailment. He left Arthurine only a veteran's pension, which barely maintained his family above the poverty line, and a salmon pink Cadillac, fully paid for.

After Stanley failed fifth grade, his mother sent him to spend the summer with his grandmother. His cousin Netta's father, a university professor in New Orleans, had promised to help Stanley with his schoolwork. The day Stanley arrived at Arthurine's house, she showed him a picture of Bubba at medical school. He was a young man in a T-shirt and panama hat. He held a toothpick in his mouth, and the way the light cast shadows between his teeth caused them to look rotten. When Netta came to Arthurine's to greet Stanley, she told him that Arthurine hated the picture because it made Bubba look like a farmer. Arthurine had no second photograph to prove she had once been married to a doctor.

Grandpa Bubba was the only person Stanley had an affiliation with who was dead. In Stanley's mind, death and his grandfather were hence one and the same. He pictured death as a thin man wearing a short-brimmed straw hat who drove a pink car and smiled, friendly-like, exposing his bad, bluish teeth. Stanley distrusted him as he would a man who pulled up behind him on the road and offered him candy.

It was in Bubba's salmon pink Cadillac that Arthurine gave Stanley his first introduction to death, although Arthurine never acknowledged this service. On Stanley's eleventh birthday, Arthurine put on a billowing white dress and matching sandals, and decided to take Stanley and Netta out to dinner at the Palace Cafeteria. Arthurine curled her hair and rubbed circles of lipstick into her cheeks to bring out their color.

Netta rode next to her great-aunt in the Cadillac's front seat, but Stanley sat in the back, perched on the removable seat arm, with both side windows rolled down so that he would not have to smell the upholstery. Stanley had never smelled a car like it. The Cadillac's odor reminded him of Arthurine's house, where menthol cigarettes, perfume, coffee and whiskey, rose water and hair spray had tucked away their smells year after year. If you entered one of her closets and opened a shoe box as narrow as a coffin, moments before you saw the sandals inside an odor would burst out and fill the room, a smell which may have hidden there for two decades waiting to be released. The car had powerful smells. Each ashtray had its own odor, the plastic seat cover stank vaguely of spoiled crab, the removable seat arm lowered with it a bad tar odor—not the rich scent of tar on a highway in the middle of summer, but the choking petroleum smell of newly poured asphalt.

The smells in the car cautioned any intruder that the Cadillac was Arthurine's inalienable property. She took the car with her even if she went only a block; she sat in it sometimes when she wanted a cigarette; and she kept handkerchiefs and magazines in the glove compartment. In the summer, she took naps in the front seat with the windows rolled down, her head wedged in a triangle of sunlight until her face turned the color of mustard, so that Stanley had to wonder how she kept from suffocating in the heat. Never, however, in all the years Arthurine had given to making the car a second home, did it occur to her to learn how to drive.

This was precisely the concern of her grandson as Arthurine, heading for the Palace Cafeteria, eased her Cadillac past the divider onto the left side of a six-lane highway. She pressed her foot on the accelerator until the speedometer's fluorescent needle paused at forty. A car approaching in the same lane from three blocks away veered swiftly into the neighboring lane and whipped past the Cadillac.

Stanley looked at Netta, trying to summon the meaning of his eleven years into his mouth, trying to taste who he was before he died.

"Arthurine," Netta said, "you're going the wrong way down a six-lane divided highway."

"Don't tell me how to drive," Arthurine answered. She slowed her car to a steady twenty miles per hour, and glanced at the other cars whizzing away from her in the side mirror. Her own yellowish face smiled at her from the window glass.

As Stanley watched his grandmother's hands on the wheel, a bitter taste rose in his throat. He thought to himself that he had no more control over Arthurine than over the car, which he also did not know how to operate. The car, like the memory of Stanley's grandfather, belonged to Arthurine, and she could twist its purpose however she wanted.

Netta was watching the road. About forty yards up, an opening appeared in the divider. "Arthurine," Netta advised with the insolence of someone who expected to be ignored, "turn here, there's a divider break."

Arthurine paid her no mind. Cars buzzed past them

without honking. Honking was for vehicles that ran red lights or loitered at green ones, for lazy pedestrians or stray dogs or wild bicycles, and not the approaching mirage of a salmon pink Cadillac plunging through waves of Louisiana heat.

Netta grabbed the steering wheel and turned it to the right. The car cut through the opening in the divider as miraculous as new life, and continued down the road on the other side.

Arthurine continued as if nothing had happened. Netta looked at Stanley with relief. But Stanley stared at Netta with awe. It would never have occurred to him to turn Arthurine's steering wheel. He felt dizzy and liberated, as if he suddenly had been freed from a burdensome superstition.

"I hate this ugly old car," he said almost audibly.

"What?" Arthurine's face appeared in the rearview mirror.

"I said this ugly old car belongs in a junkyard."

Arthurine pulled into the Palace Cafeteria without answering her grandson. Except for acknowledging her relationship by paying for the children's meals, Arthurine made no gesture which indicated she was aware of Stanley and Netta's presence. She focused on a far point of horizon, just beyond the third row of tables in the cafeteria. When Stanley's lemon pie arrived with a horsefly embedded in the buckskin-colored meringue, she did not call over the waitress and order him a fresh piece.

On the trip home, Arthurine drove down the same side of the highway on which she and the children had come most of the way. When they reached the first bend in the road, the Cadillac snagged its fin on the chrome siding of a blue car traveling next to them, and bent the metal stripping from the hindmost to the front edge of the vehicle. The man behind the wheel was so close Stanley could see the individual hairs of his mustache arching over his mouth. The man's mouth was open in an O-shape, like a ghost in a picture book.

"You just scratched that man's car," Netta said. "From one end to the other."

"I did not," Arthurine answered. She drove off the highway onto the road home and continued for almost ten blocks. The blue car shadowed them the whole way. When they came to a stoplight, Arthurine leaned her head out the window. The man may have thought she was going to call something out to him, but her eyes were directed toward a house across the street.

Stanley and Netta saw a girl of around seventeen in an island-green dress, sitting on her front steps and eating a honeydew melon, her legs spread to catch the pulp and rinds. She did not have on any underwear.

Arthurine looked at Netta and muttered in a tone indicating this piece of wisdom would serve as a lifeline in the hard years ahead: "That girl should have more sense than to let herself be fucked by the eyes of every piece of trash passing down her street." Arthurine returned to driving.

Stanley and Netta both stared at Arthurine thunderstruck. They had never heard an adult utter the word that longed to slip through their mouths as easily as the word *no*. If Arthurine had talked in her coffin in the middle of her own funeral, the children would not have been half as impressed. For a moment, Netta and Stanley forgot about the blue car trailing them like a bloodhound. When they turned around to get another glimpse of the woman in the green dress, Stanley and Netta saw Arthurine had picked up speed, leaving the man's car fifty yards behind her.

Stanley found himself hoping that Arthurine would go on racing down the highway, police sirens lighting up behind her. Years later, when Stanley borrowed Arthurine's Cadillac for a three-day joyride—an event which ended with her sending him to stay with Netta's grandmother—this moment on the highway would return to him. He would recall Arthurine smiling at the black road ahead of her, the wind in her hair, and ask himself not what drove people to break the law, but how it was possible that some human beings could pass an entire lifetime without ever committing a crime.

When the woman in the green dress disappeared from view, Netta regained her composure and told Arthurine, "You have to stop." Netta added, with clear interest in the possibility, "You'll be put in jail for a hit and run."

Arthurine pulled the Cadillac into a vacant lot. Stanley watched the blue car follow them, sniffing their taillights. A young man stepped out of it onto the sidewalk to talk as Arthurine and the children emerged from the Cadillac. The man wore a straw hat and had crooked teeth. His cheeks were gaunt and pale. His face was so filled with expectancy that he reminded Arthurine of an insurance man or debt collector, come to demand his due.

She smiled at the man with a look which startled Stanley, and which would haunt Netta throughout her womanhood, a look at once helpless and coy that revealed Arthurine to be the very opposite of what she was. "*I* won't make you pay for my car if you've hurt it," she told the man.

"Arthurine," Netta intervened. "How can you tell him he hurt our car?"

Arthurine turned toward Stanley and the Cadillac, her face resettling into its accustomed expression of a tough old bird, her back to the man as she said, "Let's take a peek at my car." The man walked behind her with difficulty, because his hands were buried in his pockets. He opened his mouth as if about to say something, then closed it.

The man peered at the side of the Cadillac where Arthurine pointed to a three-year-old scratch bordered with rust. When he saw that the man was not going to say anything, Stanley wanted to shout, "But, Arthurine, you ran into him!"

Stanley barely hid his jubilance as he traced a scratch on the blue car with a detective's accuracy. "There's no way he could have done that," Stanley said to himself. "Unless he backed up in the middle of doing forty on the highway."

Arthurine pinched him midway down his ribs, and Netta told her, loud enough for the man to hear, "Don't pinch Stanley."

The man walked behind the Cadillac to write down the license number on a ragged square of paper, but saw the plates were ten years old. He tugged at his hat so that it slid forward, hiding his face. He stared at the Cadillac for a minute, and then stuck the paper back in his pocket, climbed into his own car, turned on the ignition, and drove away. Not once in the exchange had he uttered a word.

Arthurine smiled victoriously as the blue car followed a pickup onto the highway. She and Stanley and Netta climbed back into the safety of the Cadillac and drove home without further incident. When they arrived, Arthurine shooed the children out of her car and locked herself in. She lay down, resting her head on her purse, and spreading her white dress around her so that she looked like a fried egg simmering on a skillet. She kicked off her sandals. She fell asleep thinking of that time long before Stanley was a baby when Bubba had shimmied along the street to her door, the new car leaping beneath him like a salmon escaping downstream from heaven.

BARBARIANS

YES, I knew Professor Henry. I, Carol Wallington, was an eyewitness to what happened on September 3, 1972. Before that, I talked to Professor Henry in person on three separate occasions, and I probably know more about the Henrys than anyone alive. I saw from the beginning the lunacy in letting a man like the professor set himself up as the guardian of that wayward boy, Stanley. You can be sure the Henrys will appear in my book, because crimes don't happen very often in Ripon.

I do not have to tell you how happy I was when I first learned that the college had hired a new professor of American studies, all the way from New Orleans, and that he was moving onto my block. I graduated valedictorian of Ripon Senior High School, and I returned there to teach civics for several years after majoring in American history at junior college. I gave up teaching when I married. Twenty-five years later, when my husband, Bert, died, I began writing *A Modern History of Ripon, Wisconsin.* I have completed 1,500 pages. That same year, I also started Ripon's only mobile library, and it's through the Book Mobile that I met Professor Henry.

Bert died from a stroke in 1960, after thirty-three years of service at Speed Queen. All through the last months, he had been plotting his retirement. He bought a deluxe camper and planned to take me all over the country in it. With Bert gone, I didn't have the heart to venture forth like that. I'd never been more than a hundred miles from Ripon. So I pulled out the camper's backseats, carpeted the floor, and moved in shelves and a reading table. I stocked the shelves with books from Bert's study and from high school and college book sales. After that, I left Bert's blue Galaxie 500 in the garage, collecting dust and surrounded by broken lawn mowers and unused tools. Every now and then, I'd lend it out to a high school boy for a hot date or the prom, but I never used Bert's car myself. I go everywhere in the camper. And that is how the Book Mobile began.

The Book Mobile is not just a library resource. It's my way of welcoming people into the community and getting them together. The night the Henrys arrived, I cruised down Watertown Street, intending to circle the house once and look it over before visiting in the morning. I just wanted to get a glimpse of the new family.

Sometimes I and the Book Mobile play a game: I act like I'm a secret agent, and the Book Mobile is one of those fancy vans done up with radar devices you see in spy movies. I imagine I can hear conversations taking place inside the homes I pass. That night, I parked across the street from the Henrys' and pretended that I was an FBI agent watching their house.

A shape moved outside the Henrys' kitchen, and I rolled down my side window and leaned out to get a better view. This is what I saw: a man sneaking around outside the light of the kitchen window, peering in. He was tall and thin, so unusually tall that there was something not really human about him—he was a strange, devilish shape.

A boy, skinny and redheaded with a lean, foxy face, appeared in the kitchen. A girl came up beside him, gesturing at the darkness. They stared toward me, and if it had not been so dark, I would have thought they were looking at the Book Mobile. I guessed they had heard something outside: they stood there stock-still, like people listening for something they're afraid of.

The man outside unzipped his fly and peed onto the kitchen window. The boy stepped back and the girl leaned forward.

"You stupid little bastard!" the man yelled. "Come out here in the yard and do what I tell you or I'll go in there and knock your goddamn teeth out."

The kitchen light jerked off and the upstairs lights went on. The man pushed through the hydrangeas, closer to the glass, and pressed his nose up against the window to see in better.

A blue light flashed once ahead of the Book Mobile. A town police car was crawling toward me, its siren off. It parked next to the Henrys'. Officer Roquefort stepped from it and crept up behind the man. The house's porch light lit up, the front door swung open, and out came a short man with a mustache, and no shirt on—Professor Henry. Two long-haired women stood behind him.

"Stay back here with me, Betty," one woman said.

"Don't you worry now, Gertie," Professor Henry told her.

The tall man leapt from the hydrangeas and ran in the opposite direction. Roquefort chased him, tackling him on the street. They rolled around together beneath a streetlight until the tall man slid from under Roquefort like a shadow and disappeared into a wall of darkness.

"Mr. Wilkes! Mr. Wilkes!" Professor Henry yelled, stepping into the yard.

Then I heard: "Carol. Carol Wallington. Get that damn Winnebago out of here and mind your own business."

I could have killed Roquefort for that. Maurice Roquefort is a potbellied old ignoramus who has never forgiven me for marrying my husband instead of him. When I met Bert, he was a good breadwinner, ten years my senior and already holding a management position at Speed Queen, and Maurice just had a part-time job driving pigs to the Oscar Mayer processing plant in Madison on weekends. He used to take girls with him and had a reputation for doing nothing to them, just being quiet and polite and scared. Even then, he had bad teeth, as well as that long ratlike nose and narrow-chested build all the Roqueforts do. He married Sadie Hompitt, who died in her sleep at age thirty-five, which about sums up the kind of person she was. I was in school with her for twelve years and never heard her say a word.

I drove the Book Mobile home. On the way, I looked into the wall of shadow for the tall devilish man, but the darkness cloaked him.

* * *

That night as I crawled into bed, I felt myself flush when I recalled Roquefort's behavior. I knew how I would have looked if it had been daylight: my nose and neck and even my hands would be scarlet. It's a problem I've always had, that I blush easily, a bright purply red that would make you think I was having a heart attack. I can't tell you how much this bothers me. I am a strong person, and I pride myself on my ability to keep my emotions to myself. I am glad to say that usually even I do not know what I am feeling.

Therefore, the way my face and hands have of flaring up is an injustice. Sometimes when I am completely unaware that I am disturbed by something, I look down and see my hands in my lap, red as flames, and I realize everyone around me has read my mind before I even know what I am thinking. For example, I was very self-contained at Bert's funeral. I didn't snivel and act like I was going to faint, or weep and wail as if I was ready to throw myself into his open grave, like Mrs. Matachuk did at her husband's funeral, to everyone's embarrassment. I didn't make myself a burden to anyone. I stood there, stone faced and respectable, my hands in pigskin gloves. Still, a vice president from Speed Queen approached me and asked if I was ill, and if I would like to sit down. I knew then that my face must be red as a drunkard's. He took my elbow in a manner which made me uncomfortable, and I pulled away.

After that night outside the Henrys', whenever I thought of visiting them, Roquefort would appear in my mind's eye, and my hands would flare up before me. Beforehand, I had pictured the Henrys sitting inside their living room: Mr. Henry reading a history book, his wife playing a board game on the floor with their small children. And then I'd imagine myself in that living room, discussing American history with Mr. Henry. He would be a little stuffy looking, tall and portly with graying hair. He would share an article he was reading, and I would show him the latest chapter from my book. I would interest him in an aspect of the town's history, and he might write an article on it, or invite me to talk to his class. His wife might envy me a little bit, because she would not be accustomed to having intellectual dialogues with her husband.

However, Roquefort had introduced me to the Henrys in a way that made me think I should wait before visiting them again. It was a pity—here I was, a resource Professor Henry would be glad to know about. In a way, I am the walking and talking embodiment of the life history of Ripon, I am so chock-full of information. I have resided in this town for fifty-two years. My father helped found a local branch of the John Birch Society, and my family bought and sold pig corn here for three generations. Ripon is surrounded by beautiful fields of red-tasseled cornstalks. There is no published piece of literature about my town I do not know by heart and cannot add on to. Everywhere I go, I carry a pocket notebook, and I write down snatches of what I hear, tidbits of information about Riponites and their daily doings. But now, instead of making my resources available to Professor Henry, I had to hide myself away for a week or so, driving quickly by when the Book Mobile and I were making our daily rounds.

In the meanwhile, I learned what I could about the Henrys. Every human being is a mystery, and every family a tangle of mysteries waiting to be unknotted. Some people in town said that Professor Henry had two wives—and a child by each. Others said that he was a lot older than he looked, and that one of the women was really his daughter by a former romance, and that the boy wasn't his—he was a foster child they'd obtained from a reformatory somewhere in Georgia. The girl had gotten seasonal work at the Jolly Green Giant canning facility, pulling maggots from corncobs. Why she would go for that job is beyond me. There were those who held she was being made to support the family, and had lied about her age to get the job. As it turned out, she couldn't have been much more than fourteen, since she did not start high school until a year later. That July, she was seen loitering outside the canning plant with the Mexican workers and the loose girls from the high school. She was said to dress like a boy.

Two people in town, who would prefer to go nameless, thought they saw the tall, devilish man lurking around the parking lot outside Moxie's Restaurant, and also inside the public library on Main Street. Some people said he was a parole officer who'd tracked the boy down. Others thought he was some kind of gangster who might be after the family.

Shortly after the Henrys arrived, the cashier at the gas station's general goods market caught the boy shoplifting: eight flashlight batteries and some false eyelashes. Professor Henry came to the boy's defense and paid the bill. No charges were pressed.

The following morning, one of Professor Henry's wives caught a city-bound Greyhound bus in front of the variety store. After that, the boy just sat on the front steps with his shirt off and grew. He would always be reading the same book—a children's book, by Dr. Seuss, *Sneeches on Beaches*. Sometimes Professor Henry sat beside him, pointing at the words.

In early summer, I was in the Book Mobile working on *A Modern History* when the boy and Professor Henry walked inside. The professor carried a funny beige machine that looked like a movie projector but which I knew probably wasn't. He and the boy did not say hello. They tiptoed by me, whispering to each other the way people act in a library. Many people make this mistake—they think I'm a branch of the public library, but I'm voluntary and independent.

Professor Henry was small for a man, not much taller than five feet, with tiny hands like raccoon paws, and baby-sized shoes. He had black hair, and darkish skin and fur in his ears, as well as that mustache. The boy, tall and spindly with coppery hair, towered over him. The boy was already at least six feet, although you'd have guessed from his face that he was barely a teenager. But the most eye-catching thing about him was how he copied everything Professor Henry did—he bent over to examine a book when Professor Henry bent over, slapped his knee the same way, talked in the same deep, drawly voice, tugged at his chin with his thumb and forefinger. And, somehow, despite the difference in their size and looks, the boy's unconscious and worshipful imitation was so perfect I thought he must be the professor's son.

Professor Henry and the boy stopped first to look at the front shelves containing Bert's books. Our best offerings are from the library of my deceased husband. Bert was a man who loved literature and the feel of a book. He left behind a complete set of condensed Charles Dickens and leather-bound versions of all the French and Russian writers. He owned every encyclopedia—*Funk & Wagnalls* and the *World Book* and *Encyclopaedia Britannica*. Each month, I choose ten of his books and group them by subject on the big shelf of the Book Mobile, directly in front of you when you enter. That month it was things on seafaring: *Mutiny on the Bounty* and *Voyage to the Bottom of the Sea* and *Ship of Fools*.

The boy lingered at the encyclopedias while Professor Henry rustled through the bin of unsorted books from college sales and studied the back shelves. He pointed to a black book on the top shelf, jumped up and down in a funny way, and said, "God almighty, look at that, Stanley, *The Khazars* (he pronounced it 'Kuh-*zars*'), I can't believe they have that silly thing, fetch me that black one, will you?"

The boy reached up a long, spindly arm and got the book.

"Plunk it down right here, you're going to love this, boy," Professor Henry said. He sat backwards on one of our chairs, set down the strange machine on the reading table, rested his chin on the chair back, and held the book cover up before the boy. "This is about barbarians." He laughed in a strange way. "Can you tell what the cover says, Stanley?"

The boy pulled up the Book Mobile's other chair, turned it around, and sat down backwards in it. He leaned toward the title, squinting as if he were examining fine print.

"The Kuh-*zars*."

"Good Good," said Professor Henry.

"The lost," Stanley read, painstakingly, like the slow boy in a first grade reading circle.

"Now try what I said. Read it both ways, from right to left, then left to right, and just say the one that makes sense."

"Tribe," the boy said.

"That's right, 'The Lost Tribe,' " Professor Henry repeated. He opened the book and read from it. I can't review everything the college students leave behind, and I was not aware of what was in that book. Professor Henry perused the pages laughing, and skipping whole sections to get to his favorite parts. He read to the boy about barbarian peoples who howled like wolves when they charged their enemies. They left no written records and killed anyone who seemed too smart, because such a person was a threat to the barbarians, who were stupid. They drank blood and spit in their washbasins before rinsing their faces, and exposed their privates in public, even the women.

The book didn't have anything to do with American history—the barbarians were from the Far East or someplace near there. I saw that Professor Henry was probably the kind of teacher who would be loved by his students, who would do outrageous things like dancing on top of his desk or dressing up in costumes, or lecturing them on subjects that had nothing to do with what they were studying. The boy listened to him spellbound, leaning forward over the table with his mouth ajar.

When he finished, Professor Henry said, "Now let's just try what we've been doing. You summarize in your own words what I read into the Dictaphone. Then I'll write down what you say, and then we'll read it out loud—and there you'll have it, your very own private essay. Is this machine working all right now? We should swipe Betty's, it works better." He pushed a button, listened, and slid the machine toward the boy.

The boy looked at the Dictaphone, and then glared at the book, for a long time, as if hoping it would speak to him. Professor Henry waited without moving, his eyes fastened on the boy as if the only goal was to draw him out and make him talk. After a while, the boy pressed a button on the machine, and said, "I think—" He pressed a second button, waited a moment, and then pressed the first again—"If I had lived back then when the kuh-zars had roamed the earth, I think people would have liked and respected me because I would have been good at doing the things people did then. I think I would have made a good barbarian."

Professor Henry laughed heartily. He played it back and wrote it down. "Wonderful. Tremendous," he said. "Now we'll take this home and read it over lunch."

He noticed me staring at them, and said, smiling, as if he liked the fact that I was watching, "You see, I have this theory that it's easier to read if you start with your own vocabulary: Stanley speaks into the Dictaphone, I write it up, and he reads his own speech." He walked to my desk and thumped down the book on it. "My nephew would like to check this out," he said.

I gave the boy a card to fill in: he got as far as his last name—*Wilkes*—and then stopped. Professor Henry wrote down the address. They were gone before I could tell the professor he'd forgotten his machine. He never returned the book.

* * *

The puzzle was coming together. Professor Henry had two wives and a daughter and a nephew. His nephew was mentally deficient, and his brother-in-law a madman sought by the police.

I went right home and called my sister-in-law, Florence Bozeman. I told her the boy, Stanley Wilkes, was the professor's nephew, and that he must be the son of the man, Mr. Wilkes, whom Roquefort had tried to apprehend. "I wonder where his mother might be?" I asked her.

"I suppose she's that black-haired lady that caught the Greyhound in front of my store. Imagine—maybe Professor Henry only has one wife," Florence said. "Maybe the boy's just spending an ordinary summer in the country with his relatives." She was jealous of my getting close to new people in town. Florence is a shriveled up old prune, but I try to see what's best in her because she was my husband's baby sister.

"With relatives who pee outside and threaten to murder people," I reminded her.

"Bert used to pee on the lawn all the time."

"Not that I remember."

"*I* haven't forgotten him," Florence went on. I pictured her undersized face with its sloping chin, her mouth puckered in a sour smile. Most people in town shop at the five-and-dime on Main Street to avoid buying odds and ends in the variety store where she clerks.

"I wonder what the boy will do when school starts in the fall?" I asked, to get her back on the subject. "I hate to tell you, but he's completely illiterate. He can barely sign his name."

"Well I *knew* that," she said. "Officer Roquefort said that when he arrested the boy's father—Ross Wilkes—the man claimed his boy was a moron. 'Like father like son' was what Officer Roquefort said back." She laughed, acting as if there was nothing small in the way she'd been hoarding all these facts for herself. "The boy's not exactly a nephew—he's Mrs. Henry's cousin's son."

"That's not what Professor Henry said. Where did you hear all this? From that girl who's the new secretary at the police station?"

"Oh, I have my sources. Officer Roquefort couldn't hold the boy's father for anything because after all, he hadn't committed any serious crime. The boy actually pleaded with Officer Roquefort to charge his own father with disorderly conduct, but Mr. Henry assured them it wasn't necessary. Officer Roquefort did tell Mr. Wilkes to get out of town, though. After that, Officer Roquefort discovered the man had a record of all kinds of crimes: mail fraud and assault and false imprisonment."

"Leave it to Roquefort to protect us all," I said, pretending not to care that Florence had kept so much secret from me until I called her. "Well, I have to go."

By the following Monday, Professor Henry still had not retrieved his Dictaphone. It sat on the table in the back of the Book Mobile, and every now and then I studied it. It was an early deluxe model, shaped like a radio, with a door you could open for removing the tape, and a switch that let you run it off batteries or an electric socket. There was a telephone jack on one side, and a speaker over a button that said TELEPHONE, and a microphone on the other side you could talk into to record things directly. I rewound the tape, and hit the play button. You would have been astonished by the things on it: Professor Henry making outlandish statements, and the boy following, imitating the professor's mumbly way of talking so that you might have taken them for one person. I wrote it all down word for word in my notebook, it was all so peculiar.

"Now, let's see, letter writing," Professor Henry said at the tape's beginning. There was a rustling noise, and then, "Now *here's* a letter. Why don't we respond to it? 'Dear Professor Henry, I am the attorney for Little Colonel Hotels, Inc. Your outstanding bills for your overnight stays there during the afternoons of October 7, 15, and 22 of 1971 have been referred to me for further action. We hope that it will not be necessary to institute litigation that could affect your credit rating and result in additional costs and expenses to you. Nor would we want to commence criminal proceedings.' Signed 'Robert Pine, Esq.' "

"What should we write?" Professor Henry asked. "What about, 'Dear Mr. Pine, if your continuing harassment for bills I have no intention of paying does not cease, I will track you down, wherever you are, and shoot your dog.'"

The boy's voice came on, speaking with almost the same words and manner as Professor Henry, in phrases which shocked me with their well-wordedness. "What about this, Uncle Manny? 'Dear Mr. Pine, your continuing harassment for bills long paid leads me to think I must report you to the president of the Little Colonel Hotel Corporation. If this problem is not taken care of immediately, I shall feel called upon to track you down, wherever you are, and shoot your dog. I would prefer not to have to take such action against you.' "

Professor Henry laughed raucously. "Magnifico, let's get writing, boy."

Later, Mr. Henry said, "How about a letter home, Stanley? Stanley? Why don't we try writing your father a letter?"

There was a long pause on the tape, and then a teenager's cracked voice, high-pitched and whispery: "Why don't we mail him something that would blow him up when he opened it?"

"Stanley, it might help to try a letter."

"Forget it," the boy said.

On another part of the tape, Professor Henry was carrying on, saying, "How do you mean, 'It's just a fat old book!' This is *Moby-Dick,* the novel of novels. How do you think the whale would feel if he heard you talking about him that way? The characters are crying, Stanley! They're crying!" Stanley laughed in the background. "Look here, boy," Professor Henry continued. "What if *you* were a character in this book, and someone spoke about you that way, how would you feel?"

The boy's voice came on. "If I were a character in a book," he drawled, "I would jump up and say, 'I'm alive, goddammit, let me out of here, get me out of this asshole book.' "

After this was an entry where Professor Henry was coaching Stanley to read a newspaper article about a bank robbery. When they were done, Professor Henry said, "Let's write a crime story. To begin with, what makes a person break the law?"

"My daddy breaks the law because he's bad," the boy said.

"Oh, Stanley, there's no such thing as a bad man," Professor Henry replied.

"There is now," the boy answered.

"Maybe we should talk, Stanley," Professor Henry said, and the machine shut off.

In the entry after this, Professor Henry began, "Then we'll do something funny. We'll write a joke and riddle book. Do you know any new jokes? Here's a riddle: a rich man decides it's time to marry, but he doesn't know which of his three girlfriends he should choose. So he gives each girl ten thousand dollars. The first one spends it all on the first day. The second one puts the money in a savings account. The third invests it, and doubles her money after six months. Which one does he marry?"

"Who?"

"The one with the big tits." The professor and Stanley laughed their heads off. I stopped the Dictaphone and placed it in the front of the Book Mobile to take back to the Henrys.

As I climbed into the driver's seat, I saw a commotion in front of the Paternosters' house. The Jansen girl was on the sidewalk, pointing upstairs and talking energetically to Officer Roquefort, whose car was parked in the driveway. I left my keys in the ignition, and walked down the sidewalk opposite the house.

The Paternosters' lies midway between my house and the Henrys'. Mr. Paternoster worked for years at the cookie factory, a quiet, apparently reasonable man with a wife and four daughters. Then one year, he and his wife joined a religion we do not have in Ripon. Periodically, members of this sect would arrive in a caravan from Madison, the men dressed all in gloomy black, and the women in lacy white outfits. I would pass by, and hear them jumping and shouting inside, playing tambourines, and babbling in tongues. I accosted Mrs. Paternoster's oldest daughter, Isabel, on several occasions to ask her about this, but she was always tight-lipped and unfriendly. In June, however, I bumped grocery carts with Mrs. Paternoster in the Piggly Wiggly and she surprised me by telling me, without any prompting, that the family would be going to a religious "retreat" for the last six weeks of summer. In July, I watched the family packing their station wagon, and my questions were answered: Isabel's stomach had grown like a hill of dirt thrown up by a seed potato.

I watched Roquefort climb the Paternosters' front steps, and disappear into their house. Then I approached Judy Jansen, a squat, square-faced girl who would have benefited from a little lipstick and a new hairstyle. She told me that she ordinarily did housework for the Paternosters and had been paid in advance to do a thorough cleaning the week after they departed. She had just finished mopping the upstairs bathroom, and was carrying some furniture polish into the master bedroom, when she got the fright of her life: a dirty teenaged boy was lying on the bed, snoring. She called the police.

Roquefort exited the house a few minutes after our conversation, pushing the professor's nephew in front of him. The boy looked bewildered, like someone who had just woken up. His clothes were rumpled, and his dark red hair ruffled up from his narrow face like tobacco sticking from the end of a cigarette. He carried a pair of sneakers in one hand and allowed Roquefort to lead him barefoot, catercorner across the street to the Henrys'. Roquefort pretended not to see me standing there. I learned, however, when I called Judy that night, that Professor Henry had convinced Roquefort not to charge the boy with trespassing. Roquefort was unable to contact the Paternosters: they were not at the grounds of the religious institution whose telephone number they had left with Judy.

I waited a few days before I drove to the Henrys' to return the professor's Dictaphone. I did not want to intrude in the middle of a family crisis. I knocked first on the front door, but no one answered. So I circled to the kitchen. The back door was propped open, and this is how I learned a few things about the Henry women.

Inside, I heard a lady's voice ask, "Do I just pick them badly, Betty, or are all men really that bad?"

A frosted-haired woman—Mrs. Henry—was mixing something at the kitchen counter. Next to her was a Dictaphone just like the one Professor Henry had left in the Book Mobile. It was connected by a cord to the kitchen wall, and Mrs. Henry was conducting a phone conversation through it.

"Buddy seemed so different and trustworthy and everything," the first lady's voice said from inside the Dictaphone. "He really took to Stanley in the beginning. And after he lost his job that first time, his work seemed to take off for him, he had every reason to be happy. But maybe Stanley's father popping up every few years to terrorize us, and Stanley's getting in trouble all the time and everything was too hard on Buddy. He just changed on us after a while. First he hardened up and got all distantlike and didn't pay any attention to us, and then he just got mean and then he was arrested. It bowled me over when the police found those drugs in Buddy's suitcase. I honestly thought he'd gotten a promotion at the hotel."

The woman at the counter nodded distractedly, but did not answer.

"Do you think that just anyone could change out from under you like that? Or was there something wrong with Buddy all along I should have noticed? With Stanley's father, I didn't blame myself for not seeing him for what he was beforehand—Ross Wilkes is a salesman and all, he's paid and trained to trick people. But with Buddy, I feel like I should have noticed from the beginning that he wasn't what I thought he was."

"Look, Gertie," the woman at the counter said. "I have to cook dinner for some colleagues of Manny who are coming over, OK? I don't know the answer, OK? Maybe it's just bad luck, two men running out on you in a row. Or maybe Buddy *was* nice, and then the one thing that could make him turn bad happened." An eggbeater whirred and changed speeds on the counter.

"What's that noise? Is that your line? Are we talking through that dicta-thing again? Betty, I don't like the way you hook that machine up, I don't want my worries floating all over the house for everyone and their uncle to hear."

"Nobody can hear except me. I'm in the kitchen, and this way I can keep my hands free and get work done while I'm talking. The regular phone's upstairs."

"I wish you wouldn't always be off doing other things whenever I want to talk to you, Betty."

Mrs. Henry turned off the eggbeater.

Gertie continued, "Oh well. It's been nice of Manny to look after Stanley these past six months while I'm straightening out my life. No one else has ever gotten him to write anything down since third grade. Do you know I even got a letter from him? It asked how me and Mama and Mama's *car* are doing, and he signed it 'Your beloved son, Stanley.' "

"That sounds like Manny. He and Stanley are a real pair. Look, Gertie, I really have to get off the phone."

"Stanley and I hardly know anybody in Reno. Why couldn't Buddy have dumped us before we moved there? Maybe me and Stanley should come back here to New Orleans and settle in with Mama. Mama says Stanley can live here as long as he stays out of trouble with the police, but if he keeps acting up, she'll send him to live with your mother in Jersey City."

"Why don't we talk on Thursday? I don't have any plans on Thursday."

"Betty? What if Buddy's not that bad at all? What if it's me? I'm so frightened of everything all the time now, that's the only true explanation. The more time I spend by myself, the scarier everybody else seems. It's like the way things frighten you in the dark, looking like something else entirely than they were in the daytime. Night noises. Shapes in your bedroom. Do you know what I mean? I mean, say you were suddenly left by yourself, without Manny, would you—"

"Listen, Gertie, listen. I want to get one thing clear. I am not breaking up with my husband, he is not leaving me."

"Oh no, I didn't mean that at all, Betty. I just meant I'm so afraid of everything when I'm alone, I wonder sometimes if I make monsters of people. Can something like that happen? Betty?" Gertie paused. "I'm right sorry for talking your ear off. I just don't know anybody here. Otherwise I wouldn't bother you. Thanks for listening. Thanks, catch you later." She hung up.

That's when Professor Henry came in, wearing a green dress. I am not making this up. And he was talking to himself. "Monster," I heard him say, under his breath.

He took his wife by the waist, but she pulled away, telling him, "Wait, I'm busy, hold on a minute." Neither of them noticed me standing by the door.

"What's the one thing that could turn you into somebody bad?" Mr. Henry asked.

"What?" Mrs. Henry gave him a blank look.

"You told Gertie that maybe the one bad thing that could turn Buddy bad happened to him."

"Oh *that,*" she answered, opening the cabinet over the counter. "I have to get some more red pepper for the gumbo," she answered. "I'm going to run down to the Piggly Wiggly." She took off her apron and left the kitchen.

I knocked on the doorframe.

"Professor Henry," I called. "I'm Carol Wallington from the Book Mobile."

"The Book Lady!" he answered. "Please come in, come in." He opened the door wider. "Ah, you're staring at this? Don't worry, please come in anyway," he said, pulling at the collar of the green dress. It had gold brocade sewn in a V at the neck opening, and more along the hem. "This is a jelab, a present from a friend, a professor of Middle Eastern politics. I always wear it on Saturdays."

He extended one of his short arms in a large gesture. "Please pull up a chair, pull it right up."

After I seated myself at the kitchen table, he said, "I like this jelab because it lets me pretend I'm a woman wearing a dress." He looked at me as if waiting for an answer.

"I just stopped by to let you know you left your Dictaphone in the Book Mobile," I told him, placing the machine on the table.

"Oh, of course, of course. We meant to come right back and get it, but we got distracted. Perhaps you'd like to keep it at the Book Mobile for us? We have another one here." He gestured behind him at the kitchen counter. "Are the batteries still good? Do you know that it plugs in, too? State of the art." He pushed the play button, and listened for a moment, adjusting a knob on the side.

"Has someone been fiddling with this?" He looked at me curiously and then grinned. "Actually, you might prefer that one." He got up, unplugged the Dictaphone on the counter, and set it on the kitchen table, saying, "Let me make sure it's in working order." He rewound the tape, and listened for a while to the voices of his wife and Gertie. The Dictaphone had recorded their whole talk. Then he stopped the tape, leaned over, and set the machine in my lap, with his wife's conversation right there inside. As if he wanted me to know the innermost concerns of his family's private life. My face grew hot, and when I looked down, my hands were red as beets.

"Oh wait, let me see it one more time," he said then, taking back the machine and setting it between us on the table. "The quality can be greatly improved." He pushed the play button, adjusted a knob, and listened again to his wife's conversation, seeming to forget that I was even there. Then he fast-forwarded the tape, listened some more, pressed the record button, adjusted another knob on the side, lost interest, and pushed the machine back toward me. I'm not sure if he realized it was still recording. But that is how I am able to tell you what he said after that, word for word. Later I played back the tape and wrote everything down in my notebook. I would never have remembered such gobbledygook on my own.

He leaned way forward in his chair, and began, "My wife—you met her?—got me these Dictaphones when I was writing my dissertation at Tulane. I used to read Betty sections of my first draft over the telephone. She would record them, and then type them up. This was in the early sixties, when no one questioned wives doing things like that for their husbands: I asked Betty to help with my work, and she helped. With a vengeance. She insisted on typing several drafts of the dissertation after rereading each draft to me over the phone and asking for editorial changes. She typed the final draft using two layers of carbon paper in order to furnish the three copies the department required. If she made an error, she would redo the entire page."

He went on and on almost as if he were talking to himself, and then suddenly looked up and seemed to notice me.

"It's like the gumbo," he said, out of the blue. "You see, I got my degree by specializing in the history of French Louisiana. When I was young, I exaggerated my French heritage a little, and so Betty proclaimed her Cajun ancestry to everyone, thinking it would increase my credibility and further my career." The professor dropped his voice to a whisper, as if he were revealing some fascinating secret. "Sixteen years later, when I no longer really care where I came from or who I might be anymore, she's still at it, cooking gumbo and talking about her grandfather, Henri Beaulieu, who hunted alligators in the bayous for a living. Now this just embarrasses me."

I had never met a man who went on this way.

"What I'm trying to say, Mrs. Wallington, Carol, is, What if at one time in your life, you wanted to be a certain kind of man, but you never achieved your aim. Instead you just became who you were. And you turned around and saw that the person you loved—your wife—was in love with that person you had once wanted to be, and not with you?

"And what if this? What if this, Carol Wallington? What if every thought you experienced, no matter how ridiculous or wrongheaded or tyrannical, was taken seriously by the people around you and carried out to its extreme? Isn't that a just desert for an egomaniac? To be imprisoned by his own subordinates in a world of his own making, long after he's outgrown it?"

Professor Henry reached out and took my hand, and then patted it. "You're flushed! Are you feeling well? Oh never you mind, Carol Wallington. Here I am talking you to death."

The boy Stanley leaned in the door, holding a comic book. I was relieved to see him. I did not know what kind of response Professor Henry was looking for. I took back my hand.

The professor jumped up and snatched the comic book from Stanley. "Oh, the forces of good and evil, moral philosophy, Spiderman, ethics! That's a good one. Is there such thing as a bad man? A good man? Now try this, Stanley, try this. The next time you meet someone, stare at him real hard and pretend to yourself that the person is a great political leader, a savior of men. And then, take that same person, and imagine as hard as you can that he's a criminal."

He sat back in his chair, posing for our benefit. So I did what he said, and it made me feel funny. First I tried to see Professor Henry as a savior of men—I thought to myself how could this little darkish man, with his raccoon hands and black hair and mustache, be a great leader? But then I saw it, the dignity in how his physical smallness brought out his actual greatness, the intelligence in his face, his frown. Then I leaned forward to find the criminal in him. And I saw that too: the seediness of his whiskers and tiny black eyes. I could picture him holding up a grocery store, or grabbing you from behind on a dark street.

"You see, you see!" Professor Henry chattered. "So much of human judgment is in the imagination of the beholder. How can a single human being by himself know if another man is good or evil?" He looked at me and laughed, as if he enjoyed scandalizing me.

Stanley laughed too, shook his head, and sat down beside his uncle. Professor Henry talked on and on like that for another thirty minutes, the boy hanging on to every word. After a while, Professor Henry's voice wound like a spool of yarn around my head, and I couldn't listen anymore. I wasn't used to talk like this, talk that stripped bare all the mystery in a person's life right in front of you. I thought he would never stop.

* * *

I pride myself on my open-mindedness. I and the Book Mobile welcome everybody, no matter how different or troubled. But I chose not to visit Professor Henry's house after that. I heard things here and there in town about Professor Henry: that he had been observed entertaining a foreign-looking lady at the Heidelberg House Restaurant in Green Lake, and also entering the Wolverine Motel with a woman in a pixie haircut. He was later seen skinny-dipping with the boy and a yellow-haired girl in the turquoise pool at the bottom of the quarry, all of them naked, and Professor Henry doing a cannonball off a rock. Every time I heard about the professor, it made me uneasy. I felt he was a man who had no rules or limits in his life, a person incapable of hemming himself in.

I saw the professor from a distance when I ran errands in town. He always had the boy with him, trailing behind and listening while Professor Henry talked in his funny way, skipping up and down and moving his hands excitedly all around him.

Now and then at the Piggly Wiggly, I ran into Mrs. Henry, always looking worried and full of purpose. And I'd see the Henry girl and the professor's nephew hanging out together on the street, the girl talking and the boy listening. Once when I walked by them I thought the girl was smoking what must have been marijuana, because I have heard that it smells like fresh-cut alfalfa, and that is what she smelled like although it was not yet harvest time. You can only speculate as to what kind of effect Professor Henry might have had on his daughter. He did not stick around here long enough for me to study them together. That summer, as I said, she was mostly interested in her friends at the Green Giant, and not at an age to fawn on her father the way the boy did. But you can guess that Professor Henry's influence on his daughter couldn't have been good.

The boy was coming into the Book Mobile every day. He would walk by my desk with a nod, take down one of the *Funk & Wagnalls,* and study for an hour, sounding out each word, and making observations into the Dictaphone. When he was there, speaking to no one but himself, his voice was deep and flowing, like Professor Henry's. It was strange hearing such educated noises coming out of a boy who looked like such a derelict—as strange as you might feel if you heard the president bark like a dog, or jibber like an insane person one evening on television.

After the boy's visit, I'd turn on the Dictaphone and listen. He talked about everything: how cicadas shed their shells, and volcanoes, and the invention of the V-8 engine. And the papers he left. Sometimes there would be ruled sheets with nothing but loops on them, as if he were pretending to write down his thoughts from the Dictaphone. Other times, there would be a whole page copied out of the encyclopedia, word for word, all in capital letters.

It wasn't until I decided to dust one day that I discovered four of the encyclopedia volumes missing from the *World Book:* the A, E, I, and W-X-Y-Z. I searched high and low for them around the table and the back bin before I concluded that the boy had made off with them.

I drove the Book Mobile past the Paternosters'. A light had been left on in the kitchen. I thought of Judy Jansen, all alone up there in that big house, being spooked by the sleeping shape of the boy. This made me feel a little spooked myself, when I pictured my own empty house, so

I took a left and drove down to The Spot for dinner. I phoned the Henrys from outside the cocktail lounge.

Mrs. Henry's voice answered, strained and angry. "Why do you keep calling? Why don't you leave us in peace?"

"This is Carol Wallington, from the Book Mobile?"

"Listen here, stop harassing us!" A girl's voice came on another extension. I heard silverware clinking against the counter.

"Who? Oh," Mrs. Henry answered. "It's all right, Netta, it's not *him,*" Mrs. Henry said.

"It's me, Carol Wallington, the Book Lady."

"I'll take it, honey," Mrs. Henry said. The girl didn't say anything after that, but I could still make out silverware noises, and also the sound of a dishwasher.

"Who did you think I was?" I asked Mrs. Henry. She did not answer. "I was calling because some encyclopedias seem to be missing from the Book Mobile."

"Oh," she said.

"I wouldn't trouble you—"

"I'll take care of it."

"You see, they belonged to my husband, Bert, and—"

"I said I'll take care of it. Look, I don't mean to be discourteous, but why don't you just come out and say it? Stanley stole them, didn't he?" Mrs. Henry's voice got louder. "Are you going to tell the whole town about it? Why don't you put it in the town newspaper?"

"I'm very sorry, Mrs. Henry. I see I've called at a bad time," I said. "I really wasn't mad or anything. I was just worried about the encyclopedias. We don't let people take reference books outside the Book Mobile, to make sure the sets stay complete."

"I'll see to it you get them back," Mrs. Henry said. "Please accept my apology." She hung up before I could say another word.

The next day, the Henry girl came to the Book Mobile with the missing volumes. She laid them on the table in front of me and said, "Stanley didn't know you had to check out the encyclopedias."

Then she took her time looking at the shelves, finally pulling out *The Voyage of the Snark*. I felt she was flaunting a kind of false innocence, trying to prove that nothing had happened to bar the Henrys from the Book Mobile.

This was the first time I'd seen the girl up close: she was the spitting image of Professor Henry, small and slippery and dark. I found myself trying to look at her as if she were a savior of men, and then as if she were a criminal. I had difficulty with the first part, so I just imagined her as a criminal. As you may know, this girl later got herself into real trouble here committing crimes of the heart, and I heard she was arrested after she grew up and left Ripon. Sometimes I wonder now how much of a hand she had in later events that summer. Even back then in the Book Mobile there was something about her I saw right off—she struck me as the kind of person who might always be lingering on the edge of a crime, not involved in it exactly, but there just before or after and, while technically guiltless, somehow a necessary element of events leading up to the crime. She dropped *The Voyage of the Snark* on the reading table, picked up the Dictaphone, tucked it under her arm, and left.

* * *

The boy never returned to the Book Mobile, and I certainly had no new reason to visit the Henrys' house. After that, I heard more than once that Professor Henry had been seen about town with a college dropout named Tina, who lived out by the cookie factory in a yellow house with murals painted in fluorescent colors all over it. Everyone in Ripon, except Professor Henry, I guess, had noticed that she was a little crazy. She sold tie-dyed shirts and had once spent a night in jail for streaking—this was a fad then. Boys and girls would disrobe and run through some public place. She'd been the first person in town to do it. She raced down Main Street in the dead of winter, right into Sears and out again.

The idea of Professor Henry and the boy haunted me in those days. I'd go to bed at night thinking about them, and wake up in the morning with Professor Henry's small, dark head with its mustache rising up out of my dreams before me. The night after the Henry girl returned the encyclopedias, I had a terrible nightmare where I was fighting Professor Henry, wrestling on the ground with him, and he kept changing shape out from under me. First he was a goat, and then a man, and then a Dictaphone—an enormous one with telephone cords sticking out from all directions. Then he turned into a goat again, and then, here's the funny thing, just as I was strangling him, he turned into Bert, and I had to let go because I could not bear the thought of losing Bert a second time. After that, the monster changed back into Professor Henry, a goat-man, and pulled a knife on me. I woke up shouting.

The very next morning I went out to the Book Mobile and discovered that its front left window had been shattered. The glass splinters clung to one another and in the middle of them was a hole: a perfect hole, the kind only a BB or a twenty-two might leave. I knew right away that the Wilkes boy had done it, in retaliation for my complaining about the stolen encyclopedias. This came to me with the certainty of certain knowledge.

I opened the driver's door, and beside the seat was a letter scrawled on school notebook paper:

> Dear Mrs. Wallington,
>
> Everywhere I go I run into people who say you have been talking about us. You hardly know us. Why don't you please leave us alone?

The letter was not signed.

I called Roquefort.

I'm too decent to try to shame him now with the memory of that call. I'm sorry to say that he failed to help me in any way.

"Roquefort," I told him on the phone. "That Wilkes boy shot out a window in the Book Mobile."

Roquefort drove right down, but once he got here, he was no help. I showed him the letter, but he poked his little finger in the hole left by the bullet and said, "Looks to me like a rock could have done this. Could even have been a stone kicked up by a passing truck."

"It's a bullet hole," I told him. "Take a look—it's perfectly round. Anyway, what does it matter whether he shot or threw a rock at the Book Mobile?"

"Oh, it would matter," Roquefort answered, opening the door and pretending to look under the front seat for a bullet.

When he'd found nothing, he pointed to the letter. "What makes you think Professor Henry's nephew did this?"

I told him, "I caught the boy stealing some encyclopedias from the Book Mobile, and I telephoned his aunt about it. The Henrys returned them yesterday. Then this happened to the Book Mobile last night."

"I'm surprised you didn't call me about those encyclopedias right away," Roquefort said. I was ready to respond, but then I saw he meant this as a joke. "We can't have people forgetting to return library books," he went on.

I ignored him, and told him straight out, "I don't think Professor Henry is the right person to get an upper hand on that boy."

"That boy didn't leave this letter," Roquefort said. "He can't even read or write. Anybody in this town might have sent you that note." He smiled when he made his last point.

"I know who wrote it," I answered. "And I want to bring him to justice." My face was burning, and I thrust my hands into my pockets. I meant to let Roquefort know I was good and angry. I did not want Roquefort to think he'd succeeded in embarrassing me. Which he hadn't.

"Wait awhile," Roquefort told me. "You can't file a complaint unless you're sure who wronged you."

He got back in the police car, but rolled down the window and said, "Knowing Bert, that Winnebago is insured up the wazoo. You come down and file a report if you like, and we'll see what comes out of it. Take care of that glass." He drove away, keeping his headlights off, and parked halfway down the street in front of the Paternosters' house, just far enough to be out of calling distance.

* * *

Roquefort's refusal to come to my aid made me long for a husband to protect me. That Sunday I went to check on Bert's grave. I brought a new veteran's flag and yellow plastic flowers for the vase in front of his headstone.

I admit, I don't visit Bert much. I don't like cemeteries, and anyway it took me a long time to adjust to my husband's death. I did crazy things in the first months. I wore his hat around the house, and I started watching "Mutual of Omaha's Wild Kingdom," his favorite program, but one I always despised. I drank beer straight from the bottle, like him, although before I'd never had so much as a shot of schnapps. After the funeral, I was drunk a whole week. It wasn't just those things. I started driving like him, pressing too hard on the accelerator and never coming to a full stop at stop signs.

It scared me at the time—I felt like Bert's spirit was taking me over in death in a way I had never let him do when he was alive. And then gradually, I fought him off. Long afterward, I came to wonder if it was all a kind of mourning—I missed him so much I wanted to be him. And something I would never tell anyone, especially that sister Florence of his, is that I have never been myself since his death.

These are the gloomy thoughts that were going through my head that morning at the cemetery. When I got to my husband's grave, I saw that his sister had already beat me there: in the vase before his headstone were gladiolas, a flower he hated. They were a little brown at the edges, and I tossed them into some bushes. I stared at Bert's name, etched on the pink granite.

Someone laid a hand on my shoulder.

"The Book Lady! How are you?" Professor Henry hovered beside me, the boy right behind him. Both of them were holding charcoal sticks and enormous sheets of art paper.

"We're doing gravestone rubbings," Professor Henry volunteered. "Just one more step in our quest to realize the power of the written word. Perhaps one of these is of some historical value." He displayed the rubbings: charcoaled leaves and vines framed the names of old German homesteaders, long dead and forgotten. But then, the bottom one in the pile was of a new gravestone: Livia Banks's, the fanciest in the lot, decorated all up and down with poems and angels. She had her monument made ten years before her death, with alimony money. I could have told Professor Henry all about Livia—how she spent three years of her adult life married to Morton Banks, and the next twenty torturing him because he left her for Connie Whist, never letting him forget her, Livia, for a single second. She was pure poison.

"You guys, you got to come see this little one," a girl called out from behind Livia's monument. When the girl emerged, I saw it was the college dropout, Tina. What was more, she was naked from the waist up, and there were flowers painted in watercolors all over the front of her, even her nipples. Her tie-dyed halter top was sticking out of her back pocket.

"Hey-ho," she told me. She squinched up her eyes and looked at something over my shoulder. "Oooh, the sun feels so weird. I wish you could see *that,*" she said to Professor Henry.

I looked behind me, but nothing was there.

When I turned back, Tina was staring at me. She

stepped onto Bert's grave, reached out, touched my arm, and asked, "Have *you* ever dropped acid?"

I excused myself then and there—I did not even say good-bye as I walked away. That was the last time I was face to face with the professor, until the day of the crime.

Of course, I kept hearing more and more about him. Perhaps Professor Henry, coming from a big city like New Orleans, did not realize how closely he would be monitored in a peaceful town like Ripon. More likely, he was merely a man who enjoyed an audience. Why else would he take such an interest in his nephew, and let the boy follow him everywhere, mirroring his every movement? And what could be more dangerous than someone like the professor, who thought there was no right and no wrong, no good and no bad?

I wondered how much the boy understood about Professor Henry's philanderings. If he knew, would a teen-aged boy even care if he discovered that his uncle led a double life? Probably not, I thought. Probably nothing, except how the professor treated him directly, would matter to the boy. And in the meantime, the professor's nephew was harnessed to him, learning all his habits.

But later I began to wonder if I was wrong, if maybe the boy was reacting against the professor, because things began to happen all over this quiet town. First, Florence Bozeman walked into the variety store one morning, and found all the shades of red embroidery thread missing. Shortly thereafter, someone went into the cemetery, and knocked down twenty of the modern gravestones. They never caught the perpetrator. To this day, the crime remains one of Ripon's mysteries. It was a scandal—it made the front pages of the town paper for days, and editorials on vandalism poured in for weeks. People thought some fraternity boys arriving early for school might be responsible, and asked the college to discipline its students better. One letter recalled the year the college had expelled Spencer Tracy because he had rolled down Main Street in a beer barrel. A week after the cemetery incident, someone heaved cans of corn into the ventilation ducts outside the Green Giant factory. A family on Main Street complained that someone was looking in their window at night while they ate dinner. I knew to the depth of my being that the boy was behind all of these acts.

Then I woke up one morning to find that someone had battered out the back and front lights of the Book Mobile, that they'd broken off its ten-foot antenna, and scratched the decal letters on the back door that spell BOOK MOBILE.

Under one of the windshield wipers, they'd clamped an envelope. Inside was a picture of a Puritan woman in the stocks, torn out of a high school history book. The caption explained that in old New England, "tongue wagging" was a legally punishable offense. Under the picture, in barely legible, minuscule letters, was this message:

> Gossiping was a *crime* back then, just like stealing or fornication.

I'd heard rumors before to the effect that I am a gossip. However, I don't see myself as some busybody like Florence who lives through other people's scandals. I have an opposite mission. I bring Riponites to life. Who would they be without me to tell about it? When the spirit of the people of Ripon fills me, why shouldn't I talk?

Again I called Roquefort. Again he came down and

examined the Book Mobile. Again he denied believing the Henry boy was responsible.

I used harsh words. "You're worse than Professor Henry," I told him. "You're going to destroy that boy unless you set some limits on him. If you don't arrest him when he does something like this, what's he going to do next, murder and kill?"

"I wouldn't know about Professor Henry," Roquefort said. "That's really not my territory." He opened a memo book and wrote down a handful of words.

"If you won't do anything, I'm going to call the state police," I told him.

"Look, Carol Wallington, calm yourself down. Maybe I have been investigating a few things. Maybe I have a good idea who did this, but I mean to hold off until I'm good and ready to move in on him."

"Who did it?"

"You have to wait to find out." Roquefort grinned when he said this, as if he got no end of pleasure testing my patience.

I did wait. I waited one whole week until September 3, when I got up early Sunday morning to change the monthly selection on the shelf over the door. I carried a box of twenty new books outside—this month it was Bert's collection on World War I. I circled my house to where I'd parked the Book Mobile. It was gone. There on the street was nothing but a rubble of broken glass.

I saw that someone must have knocked in the side window in order to hot-wire the camper. I can't tell you how terrible it was to see that glass: I felt as if the breath had been sucked out of me, as if I was a frail, empty shell.

I actually shook: my hands trembled, and then my arms, and my legs would not hold me up. The box of books fell from my arms, and I sat down on the curb and put my head between my knees.

It took me a long time to get up and collect myself. I opened my garage and looked at Bert's blue Galaxie 500. I pulled the lawn mowers and Bert's work bench out from behind it. Opening the door of Bert's car filled me with dread. The Galaxie 500 belonged to another life where I'd shared everything with Bert. He had driven me to Kiwanis functions, and American Legion galas in it. I liked to think of the car as no longer in working order—its doors rusted closed, the motor choked up, the gas tank long empty. But the high school boys I'd loaned it out to had kept it tuned up. When I sat in the front seat, the car coughed a little, and started. I backed out of the driveway.

If the Book Mobile was still in town, I knew I'd find it, because Ripon is not big and I know every nook and cranny of my hometown. But if a thief had taken the Book Mobile beyond the city limits, I was lost. I drove up Watertown Street. All the houses looked gloomy and sinister, brimming with darkness in the early morning air. A solitary light burned at the Paternosters', hiking up their electric bill. All the lights at the Henrys' house were off, although the front door was wide open—no doubt it had been left that way all night, in the careless fashion of Professor Henry.

I turned right, drove up to the high school, then searched all of Ripon's residential area, keeping an eye out for the Book Mobile. I drove down the highway to Union Street, and up the hill to the college, and finally onto Main Street, which terminates right at the police station.

No one was on Main Street, except a lone member of the town's motorcycle gang, the Zodiacs, chugging slowly toward me. His bike made a choking sound and stopped, and he got off and kicked it before bending over in his psychedelic vest to look at the motor. With the motorcycle shut off, Main Street fell into a hush. I saw for the first time how shabby and depressed the town was: it was just a handful of blocks with a few scanty stores. There wasn't even a department store or a coffee shop or a decent-sized bank. Even Sears isn't a real store—it's just a room full of catalogs where you can send away for things.

I had no intention of going to the police station. When I reached the end of Main Street, I made a right. I drove across the railroad tracks, and circled the deserted areas around the Speed Queen and the Jolly Green Giant. Then I headed toward the cookie factory.

Rippin' Good Cookies is a big ugly building, mustard colored with metal barrels filled with lard lined up in front of it. Not really the way you'd think a cookie-making place might look. I smelled the factory before I saw it. On a windy day, you can smell it from half a mile. Even on a Sunday morning like this one, the aroma lingered in the air: a sweet, nauseating odor of baking lard and flour.

At first, I did not see anyone as I approached Rippin' Good Cookies. Bert's Galaxie 500 nosed deep into the center of the smell.

An empty green-and-white-striped lard barrel rolled into the street from beside the factory, as if thrown. "Go to hell! You just go to hell!" ripped through the air. I drove on, and there, in front of the cookie factory, a drama spun itself out before me.

Professor Henry was there, and the boy, and the tall,

devilish man who I had seen at the Henrys' that first night I went to greet them—Wilkes. Behind them was the Book Mobile, with all its doors wide open. I got out of the car.

Wilkes had the boy's arms pinned up cruelly behind his back, and was shoving him against the Book Mobile's side. Wilkes was a frightening man, with his long, thin limbs that made me think of some dangerous insect. The boy was kicking backwards at his father, who tightened his hold, jerking his hands upwards so that the boy stopped moving. Then just as quickly, Wilkes let go, and laughed.

Professor Henry lay stretched out on the ground. His shirt was all untucked and ripped, exposing a darkish chest covered with fur from the neck right down to the pants line. He was holding his head with his hands and groaning.

"Stanley, boy, where are you?" he asked, sitting up. "I'm not much of a fighter, Stanley, you could have pushed me half that hard." He stood and brushed himself off.

Wilkes took a step forward, and for the first time, I saw a rifle tucked halfway under the front seat of the Book Mobile, its nozzle pointing outward, just within Wilkes's reach.

"It was nice of you to try to get Stanley to talk to his daddy, Mr. Professor," Wilkes said. "But it's time you let me handle my own son. It's time you stop taking him around, filling his head with evil ideas and introducing him to girls with their titties hanging out all over the place."

The boy slipped behind Wilkes and groped under the front seat of the van.

"Leave it!" Wilkes yelled, lunging toward Stanley.

The boy ducked down and sideways, and when he uprighted himself, he was holding the rifle. He stepped back, raised the gun, and leveled it at his father.

"Stay the hell away from us!" the boy cried. "I'll kill you! I'll kill you if you come nearer."

"Give me Netta's rifle, Stanley," Professor Henry said.

Stanley told him, "He stole the rifle from your garage! Stop acting like he's not dangerous! I told you he's dangerous!" The boy lowered the gun, but he held on to it. "I'll give it to you when I'm done with it."

"Stanley, why don't we all sit down like men and talk this thing out?"

The boy shrieked in a high-pitched voice, not at all like the one I'd heard him use around the professor in the past: "You don't take me seriously! You don't take me seriously! Don't you hear what I'm saying?" He turned his back on Professor Henry, and pointed the gun at Wilkes's midsection.

"Go 'head! Go 'head, boy." Wilkes smiled. "You really going to blow my insides out with a BB gun?" Wilkes leaned against the van, crossing his arms and cocking his head like he was posing for a picture.

Blue police lights flickered behind me, but I did not turn around.

The boy fired.

Wilkes leapt and shook his hand as if he'd been hit, and then he cursed, "Shit, stings like a bee, stings like a bee. You've gone and lost your mind, Stanley."

Stanley raised the gun and aimed it at Wilkes's head.

"I've got him, Stanley," Roquefort's voice said. He stepped past me from behind, his revolver drawn and pointing at Wilkes. "Don't go putting his eye out with those pellets."

When Stanley saw the revolver, he lowered his gun.

Wilkes sprang onto the top of the Book Mobile in a

strange, terrible way, the way only a man who was too light and too tall like himself could have managed. For a moment, he stood still as a statue looking down on us. Then he leapt to the ground behind the van and took off around the cookie factory with Roquefort chasing.

The boy raised the rifle and fired at Wilkes, but the gun was empty and made a tinny sound.

"Stanley," Professor Henry said. "Please hand me Netta's BB gun."

The boy grabbed the rifle by the barrel and threw it hard at the side of the Book Mobile. The dent is still there, right under the hole made by the BB that skinned Wilkes's hand. Stanley turned back to Professor Henry and said, "You tried to make me stop and talk to him! You could have protected me, but you didn't. You didn't even listen to me." He picked up the rifle from the asphalt and walked away from us, toward the railroad tracks.

Roquefort called me that afternoon, and asked me to come to the station. When I kept my appointment, I learned that Roquefort had Wilkes there. Roquefort wanted to charge him with grand larceny, and needed me to testify that the Winnebago belonged to me, and that Wilkes had taken it without my permission. Roquefort thought he could charge Wilkes with vandalism for the damage he'd done to my ignition when he hot-wired the Book Mobile, too. In return, I'd get all the information that interested me.

Roquefort told me that Wilkes had been harassing the Henrys with phone calls for weeks, threatening blackmail and even bodily harm if they didn't give him the boy. The Henrys had thought the calls were coming from out of state. They weren't. All that summer since the Henrys had moved in, Wilkes was staying right in town.

And this was the terrible story at the heart of things. At first, Wilkes had checked into the Wolverine Motel. But after the boy was caught sleeping at the Paternosters', Wilkes had learned the house was empty, and he'd moved in there. He slept in the Paternosters' beds, and sat in their chairs. He bathed in their tub, and soaked in Isabel Paternoster's scented milk bath. He used up their shampoo and their last soap bar. And he ate their food: he opened the basement freezer, and found the venison and flank steaks and ate them. He ate all the rice and beans and other staples, too, and then the nonperishables, down to the last can of pears and the last tin of sardines.

All that time, he was watching the boy from the Paternosters' windows, sometimes leaving the house at night to follow him and wander around town, asking about him. A regular at the public library remembered having talked to Wilkes, and so did a waitress at the A & W. On September 3, Wilkes stole the Book Mobile and headed toward the dropout Tina's house near the cookie factory, apparently expecting to find the professor and Stanley out there, maybe planning to abscond with the boy. Wilkes cut off Stanley and the professor with the Book Mobile while they were heading back from Tina's across the factory grounds.

Roquefort told me he'd suspected all along that Wilkes had never left town, but smoked him out of the Paternosters' house only after I'd called the second time about the Book Mobile. "I'm not exactly sure why he was doing it," Roquefort finally said, leading up to his concluding insult, "but it was Wilkes leaving those messages for you at the

Book Mobile. He wrote that second one on a page he tore out of an old textbook from the town library. Maybe he'd been spying on you from the Paternosters' house and resented you for snooping around in the same territory where he was snooping."

The following day, I did a crazy thing. I drove the Book Mobile all the way to the north end of Lake Winnebago, and then traveled east to Manitowoc, and from there, angled south along the Great Lake toward Sheboygan. By evening, I'd journeyed almost one hundred miles from Ripon. When I hit the hundred-mile mark on the odometer, my heart was fluttering like a flag in the wind. I decelerated and parked on the road shoulder. I got out of the Book Mobile and set my feet on the ground. It was like standing on the edge of the world: before me, Lake Michigan stretched out, flat and endless like a gray cornfield, the way I imagine oceans must look.

Behind me were the barbarians. I saw with perfect clarity that the Henrys were outsiders in the deepest sense, that they had settled in our midst but did not belong in Ripon and never would. They were wilder than us, and more full of life, and more dangerous. With this dark thought in my mind, I climbed back into the Book Mobile, swung it in a U-turn, and barreled home.